"I went outside to check on the horses," Karina continued after she'd gathered her breath. "When I stepped into the barn, he hit me over the head. I didn't even see him. Didn't know he was there until it was too late."

Cord jumped right on that. "But you could tell for sure that it was a man?"

"Yes," she said without hesitation.

Damn. "What happened next?" he pressed when she didn't continue.

Karina closed her eyes a moment. Shuddered. "I screamed as I was falling, and he cut my face." She reached to put her fingers there, but the paramedic moved them away.

It was the slice on her cheekbone. And the signature of the Moonlight Strangler.

LAYING DOWN THE LAW

USA TODAY Bestselling Author

DELORES FOSSEN

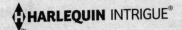
HARLEQUIN INTRIGUE®

Recycling programs
for this product may
not exist in your area.

ISBN-13: 978-0-373-69926-1

Laying Down the Law

Copyright © 2016 by Delores Fossen

This is a work of fiction. Names, characters, places and incidents are either the product of the author's imagination or are used fictitiously, and any resemblance to actual persons, living or dead, business establishments, events or locales is entirely coincidental.

This edition published by arrangement with Harlequin Books S.A.

For questions and comments about the quality of this book, please contact us at CustomerService@Harlequin.com.

® and TM are trademarks of Harlequin Enterprises Limited or its corporate affiliates. Trademarks indicated with ® are registered in the United States Patent and Trademark Office, the Canadian Intellectual Property Office and in other countries.

Printed in U.S.A.

HARLEQUIN®
www.Harlequin.com

Delores Fossen, a *USA TODAY* bestselling author, has sold over fifty novels with millions of copies of her books in print worldwide. She's received a Booksellers' Best Award and an RT Reviewers' Choice Best Book Award. She was also a finalist for a prestigious RITA® Award. You can contact the author through her website at deloresfossen.com.

Books by Delores Fossen

Harlequin Intrigue

Appaloosa Pass Ranch

Lone Wolf Lawman
Taking Aim at the Sheriff
Trouble with a Badge
The Marshal's Justice
Six-Gun Showdown
Laying Down the Law

Sweetwater Ranch

Maverick Sheriff
Cowboy Behind the Badge
Rustling Up Trouble
Kidnapping in Kendall County
The Deputy's Redemption
Reining in Justice
Surrendering to the Sheriff
A Lawman's Justice

HQN Books

The McCord Brothers

Texas on My Mind
Lone Star Nights

Visit the Author Profile page at Harlequin.com for more titles.

CAST OF CHARACTERS

Cord Granger—A tough DEA agent who believes his birth father is a notorious serial killer, the Moonlight Strangler, but Cord's quest for justice puts him on a collision course with danger and a woman who believes his birth father is an innocent man.

Karina Southerland—The last thing she needs is to feel an attraction for Cord, the hot cowboy lawman who's gunning for someone she loves, but Cord is also the one person who can save her from a killer.

Willie Lee Samuels—Cord's birth father, who's in jail and charged with being the Moonlight Strangler.

Rocky Finney—Karina's ranch hand, who has plenty of secrets, and one of those secrets could be the reason Karina's in danger.

Harley Kramer—This businessman wants nothing more than for Karina to drop charges against him for breaking and entering. But how far would he go to force her to back down?

DeWayne Stringer—A cattle baron who's had run-ins with Karina and Willie Lee for years. Did he frame Willie Lee for the murders?

Chapter One

Blood.

Special Agent Cord Granger's stomach tightened into a knot.

Since he'd worked for the Drug Enforcement Administration for the past nine years now, he'd seen plenty of blood before at various crime scenes. And a lot more of it than the drops that were here on the floor of the barn.

But this wasn't any ordinary crime scene.

There shouldn't be blood here because there shouldn't be a victim.

Cord cursed under his breath and caught the eye of Sheriff Jericho Crockett, no doubt one of the first responders to the small ranch in Appaloosa Pass. This was the sheriff's jurisdiction. Jericho normally doled out glares and hard looks to Cord, but tonight he just lifted an eyebrow.

Cord lifted one of his own and felt that knot tighten even more.

"Miss Southerland insisted on seeing you," Jericho

told Cord. "Said she wouldn't get in the ambulance until you got here."

Yeah, Jericho had relayed something similar about Karina Southerland when he'd phoned Cord about twenty minutes earlier. Jericho had asked him to come to the rental house on a local ranch and had rattled off the address. As an agent, Cord got plenty of bad calls in the middle of the night, some even from local sheriffs, but this one wasn't DEA-related.

This one was, well, personal.

"Karina said it was the Moonlight Strangler who attacked her?" Cord asked the sheriff.

Jericho nodded. "The guy had on a ski mask, came at her from behind. It fits the MO, too." He glanced up at the night sky, where there was a full moon.

The glancing hadn't been necessary, though. A full moon was always a reminder of murder. That could happen when a person had a personal connection to a vicious serial killer known as the Moonlight Strangler.

And when the killer was Cord's biological father.

It didn't matter that Cord didn't personally know the man. Though they had met. In a way. When Cord had been on the receiving end of the Moonlight Strangler's knife only a month ago. But because the Moonlight Strangler had pumped him full of drugs, Cord didn't have many memories of the incident at all.

Only the scars.

And while Cord would never—*never*—think of that snake as his father, they would always share the same blood.

"How bad is Karina hurt?" Cord added.

Jericho hitched his thumb to the rear of the barn. "See for yourself. It's not nearly as bad as it could have been."

True. She could be dead. "Did she say how she got away from...her attacker?"

"Oh, she's got plenty to say. Thought you'd want to hear it for yourself so you can try to make sense of it." Jericho paused. "Is there any sense to be made from this?"

Cord hoped there was. But he wasn't seeing it so far.

"The sooner you talk to her," Jericho continued, "the sooner she'll be in that ambulance so I can get the CSIs in here to examine the place."

Cord wanted that, as well. Because the CSIs had to find something, *anything.*

Making sure he didn't step on the blood or any other item that could possibly be evidence, Cord made his way toward the two paramedics who weren't looking any happier about this situation than Jericho or him. The ambulance was parked at the front of the barn, the red lights still on and slashing through the night. That alone spiked his adrenaline and so did the fear of what he might see when he spotted the woman on the floor by some stacked hay bales.

Karina Southerland.

Over the past month he'd met with her at least a dozen times. In those confrontations—and they were confrontations, all right—she'd been intense but composed.

There wasn't much left of that composure now.

Her dark brown hair was a tangled mess, strands of it sticking to the perspiration on her face. No jeans and working cowboy boots as she'd worn during their previous meetings. Tonight, she had on just an over-size plain white T-shirt that she was obviously using as a nightgown. It was cut low enough at the neck that he could see the bruises there. She had bruises on her knees, too, and scrapes and nicks on her hands that looked like defensive wounds.

And there was the blood, of course.

A smear of it was still on her left cheek, which one of the paramedics was tending. Another cut on her left arm. She had yet another small one near her shoulder.

Along with the two paramedics, there was a third guy with graying brown hair. Lanky to the point of being scrawny, he was pacing just outside the rear entrance of the barn. The guy was chewing on his left thumbnail, had a cell phone gripped in his right hand and was tossing some very concerned glances at Karina. He was in his fifties, and it looked as if he'd dressed in a hurry. No boots, just his socks. But there was a gun tucked at an angle in the waist of his baggy jeans.

"Who are you?" Cord asked the guy right off.

He stopped chewing on his thumbnail long enough to answer. "Rocky Finney. I'm a ranch hand here. You need to help Karina."

"He works for me," Karina volunteered. "And he saved my life."

Cord stared at Rocky to let him know he wanted

a lot more details than the ranch hand had just doled out to him.

"I was sleeping in the bunkhouse." Rocky glanced at the small barn-shaped building about twenty yards from the main house. Such that it was. The *main house* was small, too. "I heard Karina scream, and when I came out, this man wearing a mask was choking her. I shot at him. I think I hit him in the shoulder. And he ran off."

Maybe some of the blood belonged to the attacker. If Rocky was telling the truth, that is.

"Where did the man run?" Cord continued.

Rocky pointed in the direction of a heavily wooded area. Which was also the direction of the road since it was just on the other side of all those trees.

"There's no blood trail immediately around the barn," Jericho quickly informed Cord. "But the CSIs will look. I don't want anyone in that area until they've searched it."

Neither did Cord. Because blood could give them the DNA of the person responsible for this.

"She needs stitches," the paramedic said when he snared Cord's gaze.

The bulky, bald paramedic looked at Cord as if he could magically make Karina get in that ambulance and head to the hospital. But Cord had less influence on her than anyone else in this barn.

"I told you Willie Lee was innocent," Karina said, her mouth tight, "that he wasn't the Moonlight Strangler." Her voice was raspy but clear enough for Cord to hear the accusation in there.

The Moonlight Strangler had been a source of contention between Karina and him after Willie Lee Samuels was identified as the serial killer. And then captured. That had happened a month ago, after he'd attacked Cord.

Of course, Willie Lee didn't know about the multiple murder charges against him yet because he'd sustained a gunshot wound and been in a coma ever since being taken into custody.

And Cord had been the one to shoot him.

Willie Lee hadn't been able to confess. Hadn't been able to confirm anything related to the dozens of murders he'd committed as the Moonlight Strangler. Or any of the other crimes for that matter. Still, Cord had been sure Willie Lee was the right man.

Until tonight.

If the Moonlight Strangler was in a coma, then who the heck had attacked Karina?

"He's your father," Karina added. "Don't you feel in your bones that he's innocent?"

"No. I don't feel anything about him one way or another."

It was a lie. Cord felt plenty. Plenty that he didn't intend to share with her or anyone else for that matter.

Cord knelt down to make better eye contact with Karina. "Why don't you go ahead and get in the ambulance? We can talk this out on the way to the hospital."

She didn't budge, probably because she didn't trust him. She'd wanted him here only so she could say that she had told him so, that the cops had the wrong man in custody. But he glanced around at the signs of the struggle to remind her what'd gone on here. The toppled bales of hay and feed. The scattered tools and tack.

And the blood.

"You don't want to stay here," Cord reminded her.

He motioned for the paramedics to come closer and do their job, and Cord breathed a little easier when Karina didn't resist. Once she was on the stretcher, they started toward the ambulance. Cord followed right along beside them.

Rocky didn't attempt to go with them, probably because Jericho ordered him to stay put. No doubt so he could question the ranch hand and begin this investigation. Well, unless…

Cord stopped that thought. He didn't want to go there yet.

Because the real Moonlight Strangler hadn't done this.

"Make sure the horses are okay," Karina called out to Rocky.

Rocky assured her that he would.

"I'll meet you at the hospital as soon as the CSIs get here and I take Rocky to the station," Jericho said to Cord. "Anything Karina says to you will need to go in the report."

That last part wasn't exactly a request, but Cord had already known it would need to happen. Whether he wanted this or not, he was officially involved. Partly because Karina had insisted on calling him. Also in part because anything that had to do with the Moonlight Strangler automatically had to do with Cord.

"You'll need to drop the charges against Willie Lee," Karina insisted.

Cord had been stunned with the news of this attack on Karina, but he was a lawman above all else. And a born skeptic. Being abandoned at a gas station when he was just a toddler could do that. Hard to grow up trusting people when most people he met weren't trustworthy.

Karina just might fall into that category.

And that was just one of the many, many reasons he wouldn't even consider trying to get those charges dropped against Willie Lee.

"Did you set all of this up to make Willie Lee look innocent?" Cord came right out and asked her.

She didn't exactly look outraged by the question. Just disgusted. "You think I had this done to myself?" Her breath shattered, and the tears came while her gaze skirted across the two cuts she could see.

There was another one, on her cheek, that she couldn't see.

The bald paramedic scowled at Cord, probably because he thought Cord was being too hard on her. If he was, he'd apologize later. For now, he needed to get to the truth, and the fastest way to do that was by not pulling any punches.

"Did you set this all up?" Cord persisted.

The glare she gave him could have frozen a pot of boiling water. "No."

Cord didn't want to believe her—it would be easier if he didn't. Easier because it would mean there wasn't a killer out there. But even if she hadn't done this to herself and there was another killer, it didn't mean Willie Lee was innocent.

One of the paramedics got in the driver's seat. The other got into the back with Cord and Karina, and they finally started the drive to the hospital.

"This attack could have been done by a copycat," Cord suggested to her. "Maybe someone who wanted to get back at you?"

If this had been a regular interrogation, this was the point where Cord would have asked Karina if she had any enemies. But he already knew the answer.

She did.

And Cord was one of them.

It was hard not to be enemies with a woman who was defending and praising a serial killer. But that's exactly what Karina had done.

"You don't know Willie Lee," she said. "And if you did, you'd know he wasn't capable of murder."

It was the same argument he'd heard from her too many times to count. She considered herself a good judge of Willie Lee's character because the man had worked on her family's ranch in Comal County for the past fifteen years. A ranch she still owned now that her folks had passed, but she'd rented this place near Appaloosa Pass so she could be near Willie Lee while he recovered.

If he recovered, that is.

After all, the man had been in a coma for over a month.

"Willie Lee's DNA was found at the scene of a woman he murdered," he reminded her, though it was something she already knew. That DNA match had been confirmed shortly after he was caught. Since it was a verbal jab, Cord waited for her to get her usual jab back.

"It could have been planted, and you know it."

Yes, he did. But there was the other match. "My own DNA is a familial match to Willie Lee's. No one planted that. I had three labs repeat the test." And each time Cord had hoped the results would be different. "How do you explain that?"

She huffed. "Willie Lee might be your father, but that still doesn't mean he's a killer."

Again, it was an argument they'd already hashed and rehashed. "Willie Lee also matches the height and weight descriptions that witnesses of the Moonlight Strangler have given over the years."

Many witnesses. Cord didn't bother to remind her of that, too. She knew. She also knew none of those witnesses had gotten a look at his face.

But that didn't explain who'd done this to her.

"Serial killers often develop a following," Cord said, going for a different angle. One that might put an end to this conversation sooner rather than later. "Groupies. Has anyone like that contacted you? Maybe someone calling themselves a fan who wanted you to get a photo or some other personal item of Willie Lee's?"

Karina shook her head after each of the questions and then winced. The paramedic moved quickly to examine her, and that's when Cord noticed that she had another cut that her hair was covering.

"He clubbed me on the head." Karina's voice was trembling again. No doubt from the fear and adrenaline. None of her injuries appeared to be serious, but the memories would be with her for a lifetime.

"Start from the beginning," Cord insisted. Because that hit on the head was a game changer. She couldn't have done that to herself. "Tell me everything that happened."

Karina flinched again when the paramedic dabbed at the head wound. "I woke up when I heard the horses. I thought maybe they were just spooked because it was a new place. I'd just moved them out here this week."

Yes, he'd known about that. Karina was setting up a temporary operation here for training her cutting horses. Ironically, the name for that kind of trainer was a cutter. A sick joke now considering her injuries.

"I went outside to check on the horses," Karina continued after she'd gathered her breath. "When I stepped into the barn, he hit me over the head. I didn't even see him. Didn't know he was there until it was too late."

Cord jumped right on that. "But you could tell for sure that it was a man?"

"Yes," she said without hesitation.

Damn. He hoped that meant the guy hadn't sexually assaulted her in some way. But if this piece of dirt had done that, it would definitely break from the

MO of the Moonlight Strangler, who'd never sexually assaulted any of his victims.

"What happened next?" he persisted when she didn't continue.

Karina closed her eyes a moment. Shuddered. "I screamed as I was falling, and he cut my face." She reached to put her fingers there, but the paramedic moved them away.

It was the slice on her cheekbone. And the signature of the Moonlight Strangler.

Or rather the signature of his copycat.

"Did your attacker say anything to you?" Cord asked.

She swallowed hard. "He laughed and said, 'This will show them.' It wasn't in a regular voice. He was whispering as if his throat was raspy."

Perhaps just someone who wanted to clear Willie Lee's name. Of course, to the best of his knowledge, there was still only one person who fell into that particular name-clearing category.

Karina herself.

Cord studied her injuries, trying to look at the pattern to see what they could tell him. Karina didn't seem like the vain type, but he had a hard time believing that any woman would allow her face to be cut so she could try to prove someone's innocence. If she'd set this up, she could have merely had the person hit her on the head and leave bruises on her neck.

Cord's phone buzzed, and when he saw Jericho's name on the screen, he answered it right away. "Did you send that ranch hand, Rocky, off to do something?" Jericho asked.

"No. Why?" ·

"Because he's not here. The CSIs finally made it so I started looking for him to take him to the office, but he's not in the house or bunkhouse."

Hell. "You don't think he went looking for the attacker?"

Jericho cursed, too. "If he did, I don't need this now. If Karina has his number, try to call him."

Cord assured him that he'd try, but he figured since she didn't have her phone with her, there was little chance Karina would remember the ranch hand's number.

But she surprised Cord when she rattled it off.

"I have a good memory," she mumbled. A comment that snagged his attention because there seemed to be something else, something that she wasn't saying.

Something that she *remembered*.

"What is it?" Cord asked, staring at her.

She didn't get a chance to respond. Didn't get a chance to explain, either. The driver hit his brakes, bringing the ambulance to a jarring stop.

"Draw your gun," the driver told Cord.

Cord did. And he soon saw why they'd stopped and why the driver had given that order.

It certainly wasn't what Cord had expected to see.

There. In the middle of the dark country road. A man. He was wearing a ski mask.

And he had a gun pointed right at them.

Chapter Two

Karina lifted her head to see what had caused the ambulance driver to give that order to Cord.

Draw your gun.

Not exactly an order to steady her racing heart. But then, seeing the man in the ski mask didn't help with that, either.

Oh, God.

He'd found her.

Cord did indeed draw his gun. Fast. "Call for backup and get down," he told the paramedic beside her.

While the paramedic did that, Cord maneuvered himself in front of her, and the driver got down onto the seat. But the man on the road did some maneuvering, too. With his weapon still aimed at them, he ducked behind a tree, probably so that Cord wouldn't just shoot him.

"Don't try to drive off, Agent Granger," the man shouted. "Wouldn't be good for your health right now if you tried to do that. We need to have a little chat first."

There were no side windows on the back of the ambulance, and with Cord in front of her, she couldn't see much through the windshield. However, it sounded as if this monster had some kind of backup. Or maybe he was just bluffing and wanted them to be like sitting ducks while he fired shots at them.

"The ambulance is bullet-resistant," Cord said, as if reading her mind. "And I want to catch this sick bastard."

So did Karina. More than anything. Not only could catching him clear Willie Lee's name, but it would also get this killer behind bars, where he belonged. She'd known in her heart that Willie Lee wasn't the Moonlight Strangler, and arresting this man would prove it.

She hoped.

Of course, Cord might continue to believe this was a copycat. He might not want to admit they'd charged the wrong man with multiple murders. Because in this case the wrong man was his biological father and he wanted to see him punished.

"There are explosives in the ditches on both sides of the road," the man shouted. "If you shoot at me or do anything else to otherwise rile me, the explosives will go off."

Karina gasped, and the paramedic didn't fare much better. He dropped down to the floor.

"Explosives?" Cord asked, glancing around. He spoke in a loud enough voice that the guy outside would have no trouble hearing him. "That's not the MO of the Moonlight Strangler."

"You're right, but sometimes a man's gotta get cre-

ative. The explosives might not kill you. *Might* not.
But it's a big ol' risk to take with such fragile cargo
inside, isn't it?"

That got Karina snapping to a sitting position. Or
rather she tried to do that. She was strapped to the
gurney that was locked in place on the floor, but she
still lifted her torso as much as she could.

"I'm not that fragile," she insisted. However, the
dizziness hit her, and almost immediately she had no
choice but to drop back down.

Karina cursed the dizziness. The pain. Cursed the
fact that this idiot was taunting her after he'd come
so close to killing her.

She could still feel his hands around her neck.
Could still smell his stench on her skin. Could still
hear his gravelly voice as he'd cut her.

This will show them.

But he'd whispered something else to her, too.
Something she hadn't been able to catch because
by then the pain and the panic had been screaming
through her head.

What had he said to her? *What?*

Knowing that might help them if she could somehow use those words to figure out who was behind
that mask.

He'd seemed…familiar. Or something.

"Do you see any explosives?" the driver asked
Cord. Unlike Cord, his voice was trembling. Probably the rest of him, too.

Cord shook his head. "It's too dark to see much of
anything out there."

No doubt part of this killer's plan. There might not be any explosives at all. But Karina rethought that. The attack at her place had happened nearly an hour ago. That was plenty of time for the killer to get out here and set up an ambush, especially since this was the only road leading into town.

It was also the same road that the backup lawmen would be taking.

Karina prayed their arrival wouldn't make this situation worse than it already was. Maybe the deputies or whoever responded would be able to sneak up on the man and capture him. Alive. That way, he could answer questions and clear Willie Lee's name for good.

"What do you want?" Cord shouted to the man.

"The woman," he readily answered.

Had her heart skipped a beat or two? It certainly felt like it.

Cord glanced back at her, probably trying to reassure her that he wouldn't just hand her over to a killer. And he wouldn't. She'd only known him a month, but he wasn't a coward or a dirty lawman. He didn't like her. Possibly even hated her. But he would protect her with his life.

But that wasn't comforting.

Karina didn't want anyone dying to save her. Still, she wasn't exactly in a position to defend herself.

"Why do you want her?" Cord called out to him.

"Because I'd like to finish what I started." Another fast answer. Whether it was true or not, she didn't know.

Was something else going on here?

"We should have started with introductions first," Cord said. He moved to the front seat, probably so he could be in a better position to return fire. "Who are you?"

The man laughed. "And here I thought you were smarter than that. After all, we do share the same DNA."

She could only see the side of Cord's face, but she saw a muscle flicker in his jaw. "So, you're saying you're the Moonlight Strangler? Because you can't be. He's in a coma."

"I'm not just saying it. I *am* the Moonlight Strangler."

"Right," Cord grumbled under his breath. Karina had no trouble hearing his skepticism.

"Though I gotta tell you, I never liked that name," the man continued. "Moonlight Slasher would have been a whole lot better, don't you think?"

"Haven't given it much thought. A killer's a killer no matter what he's called. But I'm not convinced you're who you're saying you are. Convince me," Cord insisted.

The guy laughed. "Boy, you got a smart mouth. I like that. It's something we have in common."

"I have nothing in common with you," Cord snapped.

Karina figured that Cord didn't want her to be part of this conversation. Correction: a part of this taunting. But this might be the only chance she got to ask the question she needed her attacker to answer.

"Why do you want me dead?" Karina shouted to the man.

That earned her a glare from Cord, and he motioned for her to get back down. She didn't.

"Tell me why!" Karina said in an even louder voice when the man didn't answer.

"You're not gonna like the answer, sweetheart," the man finally said.

The *sweetheart* turned her stomach. He'd used that same syrupy tone when he'd been attacking her.

Except he had used a different tone when he'd mumbled those handful of words that she hadn't understood.

"Besides," the man went on, "talking time is over now. I figure Sheriff Jericho Crockett or his lawmen brothers are trying to sneak up on me right about now. Hope they don't step on anything that'll make 'em go ka-boom." He laughed. "Oh, wait. I do hope that happens. Crockett blood spilled all over these woods. What a nice way to end the night."

Oh, mercy. "You have to warn Jericho," she told Cord.

Cord motioned for the ambulance driver to make another call. The man did, and he told whoever answered that there might be explosives not just in the ditches, but also in the woods. Hopefully, the lawmen would get the word in time.

"Time's up," the man yelled. "Hate to sound all dramatic, but hand her over or else."

"She's hurt," Cord answered. "And I'm sure you

know why since you're the one who hurt her. She can't walk."

"Liar. I didn't do a damn thing to her legs."

"It's her head," Cord explained. "You hit her hard enough that you might have fractured her skull. That's why she's in an ambulance on the way to the hospital."

Silence.

For a long time.

So long that Karina got a really bad feeling. A feeling that went all the way to her bones. If she didn't do something fast, he was either going to kill them all or get away.

"Cord can carry me to you," she told the man.

As expected, that really didn't go over very well with Cord. "Have you lost your mind?" he snarled.

Possibly. She didn't have a fractured skull, as Cord had told her attacker, but she was dizzy and in pain. Still, this might be their only shot at catching the man. After all, he'd have to come out of his hiding place to get to her.

"He doesn't want to shoot me," she whispered to Cord. "If he did, he would have done that in the barn."

Cord's eyes narrowed. "A bullet isn't the only way to kill you."

She was well aware of it and touched her fingers to her neck to let him know that. "If you're carrying me, he won't shoot. And once you're close enough to him, you can drop me and grab him."

Cord cursed. "There are about a dozen things that could go wrong with a stupid plan like that—

including he could kill us both and then come after the paramedics to kill them, too. Is that what you want?"

Karina didn't get a chance to answer that because her attacker ducked out of sight behind the tree.

"Too late," the man shouted.

"Get down!" Cord warned them, and he moved back to the gurney to cover her body with his.

Not a second too soon.

The blast tore through the ambulance, tossing it and shaking the ground beneath them.

It was deafening.

And then everything happened much too fast for Karina to process a lot of it. They were moving, tumbling. Crashing into things.

Debris, flying everywhere.

Somehow, Cord managed to keep hold of her, and since the gurney was anchored to the floor, he was toppled around with her. No way to brace herself, no way to do anything but wait for this nightmare to end and pray they stayed alive.

There was the sound of metal screeching against the pavement, and the ambulance finally stopped with a jolting thud.

What had happened now?

And was everyone okay?

The ambulance was a jumbled mess, and it took her a moment to realize it was on its side. That was likely where the impact had landed him.

"He set off the explosives," she said. Though Cord had obviously already figured that out.

There was a cut on his forehead and some blood in his light brown hair. Heaven knew where else he was hurt, but at least he wasn't moaning in pain like the bald paramedic crumpled next to them.

"Are you all right?" Cord asked her.

No. Not by a long shot. But Karina didn't think she'd gotten any other injuries, probably because she'd been held in place on the gurney. And because of Cord.

"I'm not hurt," she responded. Maybe that was true, but everything inside her felt bruised and raw.

Cord pulled the straps off her and eased her sideways off the gurney and onto the floor. "Help him," Cord told her.

That's when she saw the angry gash on the bald paramedic's head. Not a simple cut like the one on Cord's, either. This one was deep, and he was losing a lot of blood.

It was hard to find anything in the debris, so she used the cotton blanket that'd been covering her and pressed it to his wound. While she did that, Cord checked on the paramedic in the front seat. It didn't help her nerves any when he pressed his fingers to the guy's neck.

"Is he dead?" she asked hesitantly.

Cord shook his head. "Just unconscious." He used the radio in the front to call for assistance. "Stay put," he warned her.

Despite the debris and clutter everywhere, Cord managed to make his way to the back of the ambulance. He had his gun ready when he tried the door handle. It took several pushes, but he finally got it open.

Karina couldn't see anything outside because Cord was blocking the way. He didn't go outside. He stayed there, his gaze firing around and his head raised. Listening.

She heard the moan coming from the front seat, and several moments later, the paramedic in the front lifted his head. "What the heck happened?" he grumbled.

"An explosion." Cord didn't even glance back at the guy. He kept his focus outside. No doubt in case the killer came after them again.

That gave her a fresh jolt of adrenaline.

They were stuck here. Right where the killer could get them. And this time, he just might succeed.

This nightmare wasn't over. It was just beginning.

"Try to level your breathing," Cord told her. "I don't want you to hyperventilate."

Since she was very close to doing just that, Karina tried to slow down her breathing. Tried to steady her heartbeat, too. She wasn't very successful at doing either.

"Jericho should be here any minute," Cord assured her.

She wasn't sure if that was wishful thinking or if he'd gotten confirmation of that when he'd used the ambulance's radio. Karina certainly didn't hear any sirens.

But then she also didn't hear their attacker taunting them.

"Is he still out there?" she asked, and wasn't aware she was holding her breath until her lungs started to ache.

Cord didn't jump to answer her. He continued to look around. "I don't see him. That doesn't mean he's not there."

True. "You'll have to warn Jericho." She didn't want the sheriff driving into a trap.

"He knows," Cord assured her. He shifted his position, lifting his head.

And then he cursed.

He drew in several more breaths and cursed again.

"Can you walk?" Cord looked at her first for an answer, then at the bleeding paramedic.

"Yes," Karina answered at the same time the paramedic mumbled a not so convincing "yeah."

"Why?" she asked.

But it wasn't necessary for Cord to answer her because she smelled two things that she didn't want to smell.

Gasoline.

And smoke.

"Did he set a fire?" she blurted out.

Cord didn't answer her question. "We're getting out of here now. Now!" he ordered, glancing back at the paramedic in front.

"What's going on?" the paramedic asked, but despite being dazed and injured, he started climbing over the seat toward them.

Now, Cord made eye contact with Karina. Their

gazes held for a few intense seconds. "When you get out, start running as fast as you can and don't look back."

Chapter Three

Their situation had gone from bad to much, much worse.

Cord wasn't sure if he could get Karina and the paramedics out of there alive. Still, he had to try because he didn't have many options here.

"Stay out of the ditches," Cord reminded them.

Maybe their attacker had lied about putting explosives on both sides of the road, but it was too big of a risk to take. Especially since there had indeed been explosives somewhere near the ambulance. Where exactly those explosives had been placed, Cord still didn't know, and he didn't have time to find out if there were others.

Cord stepped out of the ambulance. Not easily. He'd been banged up when they'd been tossed around. No broken bones, thank God, but he'd have bruises, and he was still recovering from injuries he'd gotten last month, thanks to the Moonlight Strangler. Those bruises and injuries made themselves known when he pivoted, looking for the idiot who'd done this to them.

No sign of anyone.

But at the moment the bomber wasn't even his main concern. It was the thin line of fire snaking its way from the side of the road toward the ambulance. The fire line was too narrow and straight to have been spilled randomly or have leaked out from the ambulance.

Which meant their attacker had set it.

Probably before they'd even arrived at this point on the road.

In addition to the smoke from the fire trail, there was white steam spewing from what was left of the ambulance engine. Normally, he wouldn't have considered that a good thing, but he did now. Because the steam and the smoke just might conceal them enough so their attacker wouldn't be able to gun them down when they made a run for it.

"Stay low and move fast," Cord told them, doubting either of the paramedics could do that last part.

He had to keep watch, but he reached behind him, and with his left hand, he hauled out Karina. The paramedics followed after her, and once they all had their feet on the ground, Cord got them moving.

Away from the spot where he'd last seen the man in the ski mask.

Away from the ambulance.

That meant jumping the ditch. Again, it wasn't easy. Everyone was limping, hurt, struggling. But Karina and the paramedics all had a clear sense of how critical it was to put some distance between them and the fire.

Cord sure had a clear sense of it.

"Try to make sure the ambulance and steam hide you as much as possible," Cord added.

They each crossed the ditch while Cord kept watch. Still no signs of their mask guy or of Jericho. Cord figured both were out there, though. The trick would be to avoid another attack before backup arrived and not hit Jericho or one of the deputies with friendly fire.

He braced himself for shots to come right at them. After all, their attacker was armed. But no shots came. Nor were there any sounds that the man was about to launch another attack. Just the stench of the smoking rubber tires and the gasoline.

Cord was the last to jump the ditch, and as soon as he was on the other side, he hurried the others into a cluster of trees. Not ideal cover since someone could sneak up on them, but if the ambulance did explode, then they'd at least stand a chance of being protected from flying debris.

"Get down on the ground," he told them. "And stay low."

Again, not easy. The paramedic with the head wound tried to muffle his groans of pain, but he didn't quiet manage it. Worse, he was still bleeding, and even though Karina was trying to add some pressure to the gash, he was losing a lot of blood.

"The killer wants me," Karina whispered. "If he has me, you and the paramedics might be safe."

Hell, no. Cord knew where this conversation was about to go, and he nipped it in the bud. "You're not going out there. He wants us all dead. That's why he set those explosives."

That was possibly true anyway. Obviously, the blast hadn't killed them, so maybe this was all part of some sick plan to get them in the open.

If so, it'd worked.

They were indeed in the open with only one gun among them and a likely copycat killer ready, willing and able to do them all in.

"Just stay down," Cord snapped to Karina when she lifted her head. "I don't have time to watch you and everything else."

Yeah, it was a jab that she probably didn't deserve, since she'd certainly pulled her own weight getting out of the ambulance. But maybe it was enough of a jab to keep her head out of the path of a bullet.

Or an explosion.

Even though he'd tried to brace himself for it, the blast jolted through his body, shaking him to the core.

The debris came bursting out from the fireball, all that was left of the ambulance. The trickle of flames had obviously made its way to the engine and heated it enough to cause the blast.

That was probably what their attacker intended.

A chunk of metal flew into the tree, inches from where Cord was standing, and he felt a sharp tug on the leg of his jeans. Karina pulled him to the ground next to her.

"It won't help us if you get yourself killed," she warned, sounding a lot tougher than she probably felt right now.

But she was right. Cord had to stay alive.

The wave of smoke came at them. It was mixed with the stench of the burning rubber, and Cord had to cover his mouth to keep from coughing.

"Y'all okay?" their attacker called out.

Cord wished he could do something about that smug tone. Like beat the guy senseless. What Cord couldn't do was answer him. It was possible the question was meant to help the fool pinpoint their location.

"Because I'd hate to think I gave any of you more boo-boos," the man added. Then, he laughed. He was still somewhere on the other side of the road.

That was the good news.

It meant he wasn't sneaking up behind them.

But he could have hired guns. And probably did. It would have been hard for him to pull this off by himself unless he'd set the explosives before attacking Karina, and those hired guns could be anywhere.

"What? Cats got your tongues?" the man asked.

His taunts made Cord's blood run cold. And made his temper run hot.

"Being quiet won't help," he taunted. "I'll find you."

"His voice," Karina whispered.

Even though he hated to risk looking at her, Cord did, to see what the heck she was talking about. "What about his voice?"

She opened her mouth. Closed it. Shook her head. "It's the same man who attacked me in the barn."

Of course it was. There'd been no doubt about that. So, what exactly had Karina meant to say?

Or rather what was she trying to keep from him?

Well, whatever the heck it was, Cord would find out. As soon as they got out of this mess.

The seconds crawled by, turning into minutes. Cord forced himself to listen through the crashing of his heartbeat in his ears. Each tiny sound put him on full alert.

Until one sound caused him to pivot in that direction.

Footsteps.

"It's me," someone said. Jericho.

Cord didn't ease the grip on his gun, though, until he actually spotted the sheriff. He was weaving his way through the trees, coming toward them.

"He's over there," Cord informed him right off, and he tipped his head in the direction where he'd last heard the guy. "Did you bring backup?"

Jericho nodded and glanced at Karina and the paramedics, before focusing on the area Cord had pointed out. "My brother Jax is somewhere nearby." He motioned toward the area just south of the attacker. "My other brother, Levi, is on the way."

So, maybe Jax was already close enough to stop him. Cord didn't know Jericho's brothers that well, but Jax had been a deputy sheriff for years. Hopefully, that was enough experience so he wouldn't walk into a trap.

"There might be other explosives," Cord pointed out.

Another nod from Jericho. "We got your warning and then heard the blast. Jax will be watching for anything suspicious. If Jax gets a shot, though, he'll take it."

Cord knew what that meant—they might not be able to take this guy alive. Part of him wanted the moron alive. Because he wanted answers. But since he was convinced this was a copycat, they could perhaps get those answers even if the man was dead. Besides, if he stayed alive and managed to get away, he'd likely just come after Karina again.

"I can't stop the bleeding," Karina mumbled.

Her hands were covered with blood now, and the paramedic was barely conscious. They needed an ambulance and needed one fast. It was time to try to end this stalemate and maybe distract the man so that he wouldn't hear Jax approaching him.

"Just how long do you think you can stay out here like this?" Cord shouted.

The guy laughed. "Well, you're alive after all. And to answer your question, I can wait as long as it takes. But I'm guessing that's not true for you, huh? Just how bad are Karina-girl and the others hurt? I didn't get a good enough look to know when y'all ran like rats."

Cord had to get his teeth unclenched before he could answer. "If you're so concerned about them, why don't you surrender and find out for yourself how they're doing? We can have a chat about them after they're on the way to the hospital."

Silence. It went on way too long. "Nope. Not in a chatting mood right now. I'm thinking it's time for me to get myself out of here. Another time, another place, Agent Granger."

And almost immediately Cord heard some footsteps. Not the light treading ones as Jericho's had been. Someone was running.

Karina would have gotten to her feet if Cord hadn't pushed her back down. "He's getting away," she argued.

Not if Cord had something to do about it. "Wait here with them," Cord told the sheriff.

He was about to bolt after the man when Jericho moved in front of him. "I'll go. My brothers and I have signals already worked out. Keep watch, though, because this could be a trick."

True. The man could be pretending to leave so he could ambush them. With Jax already out there somewhere, Cord didn't want him to get caught in friendly fire.

Jericho headed out, hurrying but threading his way through the trees to keep his cover. Cord figured Jericho wouldn't cross the road until he was clear of all the debris from the burning ambulance. Or until he was sure this clown wouldn't spot him and shoot him.

All Cord could do was wait.

The paramedic who'd been driving took off his shirt and moved closer to Karina so he could help with his bleeding partner. Cord tuned them out and listened. No more running footsteps, but he did hear something. A sort of loud pop.

Karina obviously heard it, too, because her gaze slashed in the direction of the sound. "Did he hit someone?"

Cord shook his head. Too bad he knew from a case he'd worked the sound a hammer made when hitting a human body.

The next sound was one he had no trouble recognizing.

A shot.

It cracked through the air in the same general area where their attacker had been. And it was soon followed by another bullet.

Damn. He hoped Jericho and his brother hadn't become this snake's next targets.

Waiting had never been Cord's strong suit, and it didn't help that he had a guy literally bleeding to death next to his feet and a would-be killer was out there who thought this was a sick game.

Finally, he heard another sound that wasn't more shots. It was footsteps, and they were heading right in Cord's direction.

"It's me," Jericho called out again. He wasn't running exactly, but it was close. And the lawman was all in one piece.

The breath Karina blew out was loaded with relief. Relief that Cord shared. Jericho hadn't been shot. But that didn't mean all was well.

"Your brothers?" Cord asked.

"Are in pursuit of the guy in the ski mask." Jericho looked up the road. "An ambulance will be here in just a few minutes."

Good. That was a start.

"You can't let that man get away," Karina said, standing and meeting Jericho's gaze.

"We'll do our best. In the meantime, there's a note for you nailed to a tree over there."

That explained the sound of the hammer Cord had heard. This guy had taken the time to leave a note. Why?

"A note for me?" Karina asked.

Jericho nodded. Frowned. Or maybe that was a scowl. "I didn't touch it because it might have prints or traces on it. It's handwritten. Or I should probably say it was hand-scrawled, as if he'd written it in a hurry. Which is a given, I suppose."

"And?" Cord persisted when Jericho didn't continue.

The sheriff stared at Karina. "It said, 'Remember what I told you, Karina-girl.'"

Her shoulders snapped back, and she shook her head.

But a head shake wasn't the answer Cord wanted. "What did he tell you?" Cord demanded.

"'This will show them,'" she said. "He repeated that a couple of times."

Cord stepped closer to her, getting right in her face. "And that's it?"

Karina looked ready to give him a resounding yes. But then she paused. "No. He said something else." Now, she shook her head again. "But it doesn't make sense."

Or maybe it was something she didn't want to make sense. "What did he say?" Cord asked.

"He said, 'You know exactly who I am, Karina-girl, don't you?'"

Chapter Four

Karina was hurting in nearly every part of her body. She felt like one giant bruise, probably looked it, too, judging from the glances Cord kept giving her from across the hospital treatment room that they were sharing. Sympathy mixed with plenty of frustration.

She understood both.

The bald paramedic was in another room getting stitched up and also receiving a transfusion since he'd lost so much blood. The second paramedic had two broken ribs, one of which had punctured his lung. He'd already been admitted to the hospital.

And then there was Cord.

Karina wasn't exactly sure what his injuries were because he had refused medical attention and had instead been making a string of phone calls. However, he looked as banged up as she did. Maybe more. Because she knew he was still recovering from the injuries he'd gotten last month.

Stab wounds.

And he'd gotten them when the Moonlight Strangler had taken him hostage.

Of course, Cord and everybody else on the planet believed that Willie Lee had been the one to do those horrible things to him, along with killing all those women. Despite the latest attack, Cord was still convinced that Willie Lee was the Moonlight Strangler. But Karina knew differently. The only thing that made sense to her was that the Moonlight Strangler had set up Willie Lee to take the blame not just for that attack on Cord, but for all the other murders.

She'd had zero luck proving it so far.

The nurse finally finished with the last of the stitches. "Wait here," she said.

She glanced down at Karina's bare legs and the blue paper examining gown she was wearing. Her bloodstained T-shirt had already been bagged for evidence.

"I'll see about getting you a pair of scrubs, and I'll talk to the doctor about releasing you," the nurse added and left the room.

"Good," Karina said before she thought it through. She didn't want to spend the rest of the night in the hospital, but she wasn't sure where she could go.

Certainly not back home.

That thought alone caused her to curse this monster. Her horses were there. Her things. Her life. Well, her temporary life anyway. And now she might not ever feel safe there again.

Cord finished his latest call and made his way to her. She was surprised he wasn't limping. Or maybe he just didn't want her to see that.

She'd only known him a month and couldn't quite

figure him out. Hurt and bitter. Determined to put his biological father away for the rest of his life.

Drop-dead hot.

Yes, she'd noticed that, too, and hated that she'd noticed.

"After you're released, I'll drive you to the sheriff's office so Jericho can take your statement," he explained. "Then, we can arrange for you to go into protective custody."

Karina nodded. This was going to be a very long night, and while she just wanted it to end, she wasn't stupid. She wouldn't refuse protective custody.

"Certainly, this attack must make you doubt that Willie Lee is really the Moonlight Strangler?" she asked.

Cord shook his head. "It only convinces me that we have a copycat or else a groupie who wants to pretend he's a serial killer."

She didn't bother with a sigh, though it was frustrating that Cord wouldn't even consider his father's innocence. "Then at least tell me they found the man responsible for this latest attack."

Cord shook his head. "Nothing. So far. But Jericho's got a CSI team out there now. One out at your place, too. They're going through every inch of it so something might turn up. After that, they'll go through your house to make sure your attacker didn't stash something inside."

He didn't sound very hopeful, though, that they'd find anything. Neither was Karina. Mainly because she didn't believe the attacker had actually been in the house.

Oh, God.

Had he gone inside?

Just the thought of that required a deep breath. It was bad enough that he'd been in her barn.

"Are you remembering something else?" Cord asked.

He'd no doubt noticed the hard breath she'd taken. Heck, she could have even gone pale, too. But she didn't want to spell out her fears to him. Especially since what was done was done. If the killer had been in her house, if he'd watched her, stalked her, she couldn't undo that. No. It was best to move on and try to work through this.

She looked up at Cord and caught him in mid-grimace. So, he wasn't perfect at masking his pain after all.

"You really should let the doctor check you out," Karina suggested.

Cord must have considered that a closed and shut argument since he didn't even address it. He dragged over a chair and sank down on it so they were facing each other. She braced herself for another round of "blame this all on Willie Lee," but it surprised her when he reached out and lightly touched his fingers to her cheek.

To the cut that was there.

Karina hadn't seen it yet. No mirrors in the treatment room. She figured that was intentional since all kinds of injuries were treated here.

"How bad is it?" she asked, though she wasn't sure she wanted to know the answer. Especially since just looking at her had caused Cord's forehead to bunch up.

"It'll heal," he said, obviously dodging her question. "You're the third woman I know who has that scar. My sister, Addie, and her sister-in-law, Paige. Of course, plenty of other women had it, too, but they're not alive."

Karina knew about the other women. About Paige, as well. She was the deputy's wife and had been left for dead by the Moonlight Strangler. However, the other person was a shock. "I didn't realize your sister had been cut."

He nodded, leaned back in the chair and scrubbed his hand over his face. "When she was three, Addie was found wandering around the woods near the Crockett ranch. Jericho's dad found her, and she had the cut then. Of course, nobody knew what it meant at the time."

No. But Karina knew the rest of this particular story. The Crocketts had adopted Addie and raised her along with their four sons: Jericho, Jax, Chase and Levi. Because the Crocketts had wanted to find Addie's birth parents, they'd entered her DNA into the databases, and there'd been no match until a year ago, when Addie had learned she was the daughter of the Moonlight Strangler. Cord had been matched a short time later and was Addie's fraternal twin brother.

Ever since then Cord had made it his mission to find the killer. Which would mean also finding his father. And Cord was certain he'd managed to do that now that Willie Lee was in custody.

"Did you ever find a birth certificate for Addie or you?" she asked, not sure he would even answer. They'd had so many uncivil discussions about his paternity. Well, his insistence that Willie Lee was a killer anyway, and Karina thought he might just blow her off.

Much to her surprise, he didn't.

"No. And believe me, I looked. The county clerk said that some home births don't get registered."

Neither would someone wanting to hide those babies. But why would Willie Lee have done that?

No answer for that, either. No answer for a lot of things, but Karina was certain she could get to the bottom of it if she could just talk to Willie Lee. He'd have to come out of the coma first, and there were no indications when or if that would ever happen.

"Addie's scar is barely visible," Cord went on. "Yours will fade, too."

All in all, it was a kind thing to say. And a surprising one since it took this civil conversation to a different level.

"I must really look bad for you to be so nice to me." Karina was only partly joking. She was dead certain she looked bad.

The corner of his mouth lifted. Almost a smile. Almost. But it was gone as quickly as it came. He leaned forward, his gaze connecting with hers, and she could see that he was all lawman again. Not that he slipped out of that mode for more than a second or two.

However, the brief change in his demeanor gave her another reminder of that drop-dead-hot thought she'd shoved aside earlier. And continued to shove aside now. Hard to do, though, with him right in front of her.

He was pure cowboy with that tousled hair and those bad-boy eyes. Sadly, he was her type, and her body just wouldn't let her forget that wherever she saw him. Thankfully, Cord didn't seem to notice.

Or maybe he did.

He gave her a look. The kind of look a man would give a woman who was hands-off. Which described how he felt about her to a T.

He cleared his throat, looked disgusted with himself. "I keep going back to that note found on the tree."

Good. A change of subject. Exactly what she needed to get her mind back on track.

"The note said, 'Remember what I told you, Karina-girl,'" Cord continued. Not that he had to say the words aloud. They were etched permanently in her mind. "And you did remember."

She nodded. "'You know exactly who I am, Karina-girl, don't you?'" she repeated. "But here's the problem with that. I don't know who he is. I really don't."

"Then why would he say that? He could have put a lot of things in that note, but he didn't." Cord paused, apparently waiting for her to will the memory into her consciousness.

When she didn't come up with anything, he huffed.

"All right. Let's try a different angle. Who would want to kill you? An ex-boyfriend, maybe? A stalker?"

Karina didn't get a chance to answer because the sound of footsteps had Cord springing to his feet and drawing his gun.

However, it was only Rocky.

Her ranch hand was all right. The killer hadn't taken him after all. He looked a little disheveled, but that was it.

The relief she felt didn't last long, though, because of Cord's reaction. She was usually the one to get his jaw muscles stirring, but they were stirring like crazy now. Ditto for the glare he shot Rocky.

"Where were you?" Cord snapped. Definitely the lawman now.

Rocky pulled back his shoulders. "Out looking for the guy who attacked Karina, of course."

"You were supposed to go with the sheriff. I heard him tell you that."

Rocky's gaze shifted to her, and he looked as if he wanted her to defend him. But she couldn't. "Going out there on your own was dangerous," she reminded him. And stupid. "You could have been killed."

He threw his hands up in the air in an I-give-up gesture. "I just wanted to find him before his trail turned cold."

"And did you find him?" Cord challenged.

Rocky's jaw muscles tightened, too. "No. But I did see him. After I heard the explosion."

That got her attention. Cord's, as well. Cord made

a circling motion with his finger for Rocky to keep going with the details.

"I'm pretty sure it was him," Rocky went on. "I mean, how many men are running around the woods this time of night?"

Maybe plenty since the guy had almost certainly had help in blowing up the ambulance. "Did you actually see his face?" Karina asked.

Another "no." Rocky made a sound of frustration. "He was wearing dark clothes, though, just like that man who attacked you in the barn. I know it was him, Karina." He turned to Cord. "I followed him all the way to a farm road before I lost sight of him. I think that's the direction of the Appaloosa Pass Ranch, the one the Crocketts own."

Cord didn't waste a second. He took out his phone and fired off a text. Probably to Jericho.

Karina touched her fingers to her mouth. "You don't think the killer will go after your sister?"

Cord didn't answer right away. "I don't know. I don't know who or what we're dealing with here."

"We're dealing with the Moonlight Strangler," Rocky said as if it was gospel.

That earned him another glare from Cord. "You need to go to the sheriff's office and give your statement. *Now.*"

Rocky looked ready to argue with that, but Karina nodded. "Go ahead. I'll be there as soon as the doctor releases me."

It still took Rocky several long moments and a few volleyed glances before he huffed, mumbled something she didn't catch and headed out. Cord followed him, stopping in the door to watch him leave.

"How well do you know Rocky?" Cord asked with his back still to her.

Karina wanted to be upset with his tone and the question itself, but it was something a lawman would want to know. "Not long. I just hired him earlier this week. But his references checked out," she quickly added. "He hadn't worked with cutting horses in a while, but I decided to give him a chance."

Mainly because he'd been the only one who had applied for the job.

"References can be faked." Cord made a sound that could have meant anything and sent another text. "I told the Crocketts it would be a good idea to lock down the ranch." He finally turned, walked back to her. "You trust Rocky? Any gut feelings about him?"

"Yes, I trust him. No reason not to."

Was there? Maybe it was because of the frayed nerves, but Karina mentally went through the handful of interactions she'd had with the man.

"He works well with the horses, but the truth is, I don't know much about him," she admitted.

That was partly her fault. She'd been so preoccupied with Willie Lee and staying in business that she hadn't even bothered to get to really know the man she'd hired. A man who was living just yards from her.

"I'll have a thorough background check done on him," Cord said. He walked closer, standing over her and looking down at her. "Now, back to the question

I asked before Rocky came in. Is there anyone who would want to do you harm?"

Karina didn't even have to think about this. "DeWayne Stringer." Just saying his name aloud caused her stomach to churn. "He's a wealthy cattle broker over in Comal County and lives near my ranch. I've had run-ins with him for nearly a year now since he bought the property next to mine. He wants me to sell him my land so he can expand and isn't very happy that I won't do that."

A huge understatement. DeWayne had done everything in his power to pressure her into selling. Plain and simple, he was a bully.

"Over the past couple of months, I've had livestock go missing," she went on. "Some vandalism. I'm sure it's his doing. Or else he hired someone to do it. He doesn't seem the sort to get his hands dirty."

"And what have the local cops done about it?" Cord asked. He used the note function on his phone to type in DeWayne's name.

"Nothing because there's never any proof. DeWayne always covers his tracks."

Cord stared at her. "You think he's capable of murder or attempted murder?"

Now, she had to pause. "Maybe." Then she shook her head. "But I heard my attacker speak, and it wasn't DeWayne's voice."

"He could have disguised it," Cord suggested. "Or else hired someone to do the job. You said he didn't like to get his hands dirty."

That was true, but there was still something that

didn't make sense. "Why would DeWayne come after me here in Appaloosa Pass?"

"Because you're more vulnerable here," Cord answered without hesitating. "You have six hands at your place in Comal County, but here it's only Rocky and you. Plus, you're distracted, worried about Willie Lee. That made you an easier target."

The word—*target*—made her want to throw up. "I was distracted at my house, too, after I heard about Willie Lee," she pointed out. "I was there for several days before I made arrangements to come here."

Cord didn't miss a beat. "And it would be far easier to get onto the place here sight unseen than it would be to get on your ranch in Comal County. I've seen pictures of your ranch. There, the house is in the center of acres of pasture. No trees, no place for a would-be killer to hide while sneaking onto the grounds."

Karina couldn't argue with any of that, and she could go even one step further with it. "I think it might have been DeWayne who planted Willie Lee's DNA at that crime scene."

Cord stared at her, not exactly rolling his eyes but almost.

"Willie Lee stood up to DeWayne, and DeWayne hates him. They've had plenty of verbal run-ins. And one not so verbal," she added in a mumble.

She hated to explain this because it might make Cord believe Willie Lee was a violent man. He wasn't. Not normally anyway.

"I'm listening," Cord said when she hesitated.

Best just to tell him because Cord would find out

anyway now that he was going to have DeWayne investigated. "Willie Lee punched DeWayne after DeWayne insulted me. Please don't make me repeat the names DeWayne called me. Anyway, it was only about a week later when Willie Lee's DNA was found at the crime scene."

"Now exactly how would DeWayne have managed to do that?" There was so much skepticism in Cord's voice.

But maybe she could do something to remove a bit of that doubt. At least she could try. "The DNA found at the crime scene was in some chewing gum. Willie Lee quit smoking a few years ago, and he's been a gum chewer ever since. It wouldn't have been hard for DeWayne to get a piece that Willie Lee had spit out on the ground."

Cord's eyebrow rose more than a fraction. "And then what? DeWayne happened to find a crime scene so he could plant the gum?"

It did sound far-fetched when Cord put it that way. Still, it was possible. "Maybe DeWayne held on to the gum for a while until he could plant it. And then perhaps DeWayne just happened to find that scene. I mean, it wasn't that far from my ranch and his land."

"Ten miles," Cord quickly declared, which meant he'd memorized all the details. With reason. It was the first time DNA had been recovered from the crime scene of the Moonlight Strangler.

Cord leaned in closer again. Too close. Probably a lawman's ploy to violate her personal space and make her uneasy so she'd spill any secrets she was hiding. Sadly, it would have worked if she'd had secrets.

She didn't.

But it also worked in a different way, too. For a man who hated her, her body certainly didn't let her forget that she was a woman. And that he was a man.

"I've been looking into Willie Lee's life," Cord went on. "He was in the area at the time of that murder because his signature is on a feed purchase in town."

She knew all about Cord's efforts to seal the deal and pin these murders, all of them, on Willie Lee. And Cord had indeed managed to place Willie Lee in the areas of several of the murders. That still didn't convince her.

Karina leaned in closer to him, too. "You're asking me to believe that a man I've known for fifteen years, half of my life, murdered women and then calmly went on as if nothing had happened. A man I trust—"

"A man you don't really know," Cord interrupted. "According to your own statement, he just showed up one day, and your father hired him. Willie Lee had no references. No past. He just materialized out of thin air fifteen years ago."

Karina knew there was an explanation for that. One that Willie Lee could give her if he ever came out of that coma.

Especially since Cord's DNA had proved that he was Willie Lee's son.

"Do you have any childhood memories whatsoever of Willie Lee?" she suddenly asked.

"None. Neither does Addie." He moved away from her. Fast. "I'll have Jericho get DeWayne in for questioning," Cord said, and he sent another text. Apparently ending their conversation about his *father*.

Karina wanted to press him on the subject. Actually, what she wanted Cord to do was remember that Willie Lee was the same loving, caring man that he'd been to her over the years. He wasn't just her hired hand. He'd become a father figure to her after her own dad had died of lung cancer when Karina was just seventeen. Her mother had never been the same after that. Had never really been part of Karina's life, or even her own life. Her mom had finally ended it all with sleeping pills.

And Willie Lee had been there to help Karina get through that, too.

"Anyone else other than DeWayne who might want to hurt you?" Cord persisted. "An ex-boyfriend, maybe?" he repeated. "Or a current boyfriend?"

She seriously doubted he was fishing to find out if she was romantically involved with anyone. "No current boyfriend. No recent ex, either. The ranch keeps me busy," Karina added because she felt she had to add something so Cord wouldn't think she was a loser.

Though he probably thought that anyway. A loser and very gullible to believe in Willie Lee's innocence.

"How about any disgruntled employees?" Cord asked a moment later. "Or just someone you got a bad vibe about?"

She opened her mouth to say no, but that wasn't

true. "There might be someone else. *Might*. A couple of days after Willie Lee was captured, a man showed up at the ranch. Harley Kramer. He said he was an old friend of Willie Lee's, of my mother's, too. But I'd never heard either of them mention him."

"What'd he want?" Cord asked.

"He said he wanted to look through Willie Lee's things, that Willie Lee had some old photos he wanted. I told him that wouldn't be possible, not without Willie Lee's permission. He left, and I thought that was the end of it." She paused. "I definitely got bad vibes from him, and it wasn't just because of his scars."

"Scars?"

She motioned to her face. "He'd been burned and had obviously had a skin graft. And I know that sounds shallow to be creeped out by a guy with a scarred face, but it wasn't just that. It was the way he looked at me. Then, I caught him sneaking into the cabin where Willie Lee lived. I called the sheriff, and he arrested him for trespassing and breaking and entering. Needless to say, Harley wasn't happy about that."

Cord added Harley's name to the note on his phone. "Did this guy threaten you?"

"Not exactly, but he was furious. His trial date will be coming up soon, and he might have to do some jail time." Probably not much, though, since the sheriff had told her that Harley didn't have any priors and would likely get probation.

Still, it must have been enough motive for Cord

because he typed something else in his notes. He was still typing when his phone rang.

"Jax," Cord said, glancing at the screen.

One of the deputies. This was no doubt about the investigation. "Put the call on speaker, please," she said.

Karina wasn't sure Cord would do that, and judging from the way the muscles in his face stirred, Cord wasn't sure of it, either. However, he did press the speaker button when he answered it.

"This is a heads-up," Jax informed Cord. "You need to keep that ranch hand, Rocky, away from Karina."

Her heart went to her throat. "Why?" Cord and she asked in unison.

"Because you're not going to believe what we found in the bunkhouse where he was staying. I just called Jericho to have him take Rocky into custody."

Chapter Five

Cord didn't know what Jax had seen that'd caused him to make that call, but he figured he wasn't going to like it.

Karina certainly wouldn't, either.

She'd practically jumped to defend her ranch hand, but judging from Jax's tone, she wouldn't be defending Rocky after she saw the photos that Jax had sent to the sheriff's office.

Jax hadn't wanted to describe them over the phone, only adding that the pictures would be worth a million words. Cord only hoped whatever they were, it would be enough to pin attempted murder charges on the man so he could end Karina's doubts about Willie Lee not being the Moonlight Strangler. That way, Cord could walk away from this, from her, and know that they had the right man in custody.

Then, maybe he could start dealing with the feelings that he'd buried deep within him.

Of course, first they had to find Rocky.

Despite being told by both Cord and Jericho to go

to the sheriff's office, the ranch hand had yet to show up. Cord figured that wasn't a good sign.

"Are you okay?" Cord asked her.

Karina gave a heavy sigh and tore her gaze from the cruiser window, where she was looking at the shops on Main Street as they rode past them. She was pretending to look at them at least. He figured her mind was really on her ranch hand and the fact that she'd nearly died tonight.

"Every inch of me is hurting," she admitted. "And I'm upset about Rocky. How about you?"

Cord went with the lie. "I'm fine."

But every inch of him was hurting, as well. Man, he needed a long soak in the tub and a handful of aspirin. He wasn't counting on getting either anytime soon.

"Move fast when we get out of the cruiser," Cord instructed Karina when the sheriff's office came into view.

Jericho had sent the vehicle to the hospital to pick them up, and Cord was thankful for not only the ride—his truck was still back at Karina's—but also for the deputy driving. With Karina's attacker still out there, he didn't want to be without some kind of backup. And he didn't want her in the open any longer than necessary.

The deputy stopped by the front door, and Cord hurried her in. Jericho and Levi were there, both talking on their phones, but Jericho motioned for them to follow him into his office. Judging from what part of the conversation he could hear, Jericho was having a chat with one of his other deputies, and once they were in his office, he motioned for them to sit.

Jericho cursed and ended the call. He looked at both of them and mumbled yet more profanity. Probably because they both looked like hell, but Cord knew the cursing wasn't all for them.

"Still no sign of Rocky, but Jax is staying at Karina's place a while longer to see if he shows up there. Any idea where he'd go?" Jericho asked her.

Karina shook her head, winced a little. No doubt from the pain. Jericho noticed, and that prompted him to take out a huge bottle of ibuprofen from his desk and two bottles of water from the small fridge in the corner.

"Help yourself," Jericho offered.

Well, it wasn't aspirin and a bath, but it would do for now. Cord exceeded the recommended dose by a lot and hoped that the pain in his head faded to at least a tolerable throb before long.

"I don't know where Rocky would go," Karina said, gulping down two of the pills. "On his references he said he didn't have any family, that he'd been raised in foster care." She lifted her shoulder. "I'm not sure if that's even true."

"It's not," Jericho quickly responded. He turned his laptop in their direction so they could see the screen.

Not photos of the bunkhouse but rather a mug shot. Of Rocky.

"He was arrested for stealing a car," Jericho went on.

Karina was shaking her head before he even finished. "I did a computer check, and a record didn't come up."

"Because he was arrested when he was a juvie, and it was sealed. But he has parents, all right. They adopted him from foster care when he was a kid. They're in their eighties now, and they basically disowned him when he was in his twenties and haven't seen him since. They don't want to see him, either, and said they'd call the cops in a heartbeat if he showed up at their house."

Jericho clicked to the next picture. Or rather the next pictures. There were a series of shots that filled up the whole screen. "This is what Jax found in the bunkhouse. It was all in a box beneath Rocky's bed."

Karina stood, probably so she could have a better look. Then, she gasped.

Damn.

There were newspaper clippings. Dozens of them from the looks of it. With headlines detailing everything about the Moonlight Strangler. Including Willie Lee's capture.

"Rocky clearly has a disturbing *hobby*," Jericho explained. "I just had a quick chat with his parents—he's not there, by the way—and they said for most of his life Rocky's been obsessed with serial killers. And that they've heard through acquaintances that he idolizes the Moonlight Strangler."

"Oh, God," Karina whispered, sinking back into the chair.

"He had other pictures in that box." Jericho clicked to the next screen. Not newspaper clippings.

But rather photos of Karina.

In them, she wasn't doing anything special. Just errands, grocery shopping, that sort of thing. However, there were dozens of them. Including some of her in the interior of the barn.

Cord could have sworn that with each one she studied more and more color drained from her face. With reason. Most of the photos were grainy, as if they'd been taken with a long-range lens. And that meant Rocky had probably been spying on Karina for days or even weeks.

There were also shots of the Appaloosa Pass Hospital, where Willie Lee had stayed two days before being transported to the hospital at the prison. There were photos of the exterior of the prison, too.

"Rocky's a groupie," Cord concluded. If there hadn't already been a knot in his stomach, that would have done it. It was hard to understand why anyone would attach themselves to a serial killer.

But it did give Rocky a motive for what'd gone on tonight.

Cord made eye contact with Karina before he said anything. "It's possible Rocky was responsible for the attack. He might have believed this was the way to get Willie Lee released from jail."

He gave her some time to let that sink in and saw her trying to process it. At first, Cord saw a lot of doubt in her chocolate-brown eyes. Then, the realization that it could be true.

"So, you're thinking he hired someone to attack me," she added a moment later.

Cord shrugged and glanced at Jericho to see if they were on the same page. Judging from the look they shared, they were.

"Could Rocky have attacked on his own?" Cord asked. "Think it through. Did you actually see two men?"

Karina paused a moment, glanced at the photos on the laptop and then turned her head away from them. "I'm not sure. I'm not sure of anything right now."

Well, Cord was. They had a bona fide suspect. Now, they just had to find him.

Jericho's phone buzzed. "I gotta take this call," he said when he glanced at the screen. He headed for the door but then came back to turn his laptop around, no doubt so that the pictures wouldn't be right in Karina's face.

That might help steady her nerves, but Cord figured the images were already fixed in her mind. The photos weren't gruesome, and there'd been none of her undressing or sleeping. But it had to get to her that someone had been stalking her and violating her privacy.

"You must think I'm stupid," she said. "Stupid to hire someone like Rocky."

"Not stupid. It's just your trust was misplaced."

Her gaze whipped around, snaring his. "Now we're talking about Willie Lee."

Yeah. No need to spell it out for her, though. Plus, footsteps got Cord's attention. Even though they were in the sheriff's office, he still slid his hand over the gun in his holster. But it wasn't a threat.

It was Addie.

Since his sister was the last person he expected to see come through that door, he immediately got to his feet. So did Karina. Clearly, she was uncomfortable with this face-to-face encounter, since she started rubbing her hands down the sides of the scrubs the nurse had given her.

"I heard what happened." Addie went straight to Cord and hugged him.

Addie had hugged him before, but it always gave him a jolt. He wasn't usually a hugging sort, but it felt right when Addie did it. Maybe there was some truth to that saying about twins being connected subconsciously, because he'd loved her, and wanted to protect her, from the moment he'd laid eyes on her.

Cord didn't need to do introductions since Karina and Addie had met shortly after Willie Lee's arrest. Or rather they'd seen each other at the hospital. Addie had been there visiting Cord. Karina had been checking on Willie Lee, and there had been that strained awkwardness that was still there between them.

"Please tell me you didn't drive here alone," Cord said to his sister.

"No. Chase is with me. Weston is home with the baby."

Weston was her husband. And Chase, her adopted brother. Cord was glad Chase had come with her because he was a lawman, too. He didn't want Addie out on the roads alone until Rocky, or whoever was behind this, was caught. After all, Rocky had said he'd spotted Karina's attacker heading in the general direction of the Appaloosa Pass Ranch, and while Rocky could be lying through his pearly whites, Cord didn't want to take any unnecessary risks when it came to Addie.

"Are you all right?" Addie asked, the question meant for Karina and him because she glanced at both of them.

Karina kept her response to a nod, and Cord could see her trying to steel herself up. Probably because she believed Addie was about to blast her for defending Willie Lee.

Addie's gaze went from the cut on Karina's face to the bruises on her neck. Addie shuddered. "Who did this to you?"

Karina shook her head. "We're still trying to figure that out. Maybe a ranch hand I recently hired. Maybe someone else."

"A copycat," Cord added.

Oh, no. He could see the argument brewing in his sister's eyes. "Or the real deal," Addie mumbled.

Karina blinked, her gaze shifting to him. That gaze demanded an explanation. An explanation Cord didn't want to get into. Because his sister had her own doubts about Willie Lee's guilt. Doubts that Addie had expressed during several heated discussions.

Addie made a vague motion toward her stomach. "It's just a gut feeling. And it might be nothing. But I'm not sure…"

"You think Willie Lee might not be the Moonlight Strangler," Karina said, finishing for her.

Addie gave a heavy sigh. Nodded. Then, shrugged.

"Some things just don't add up, that's all. Months ago, not long after I found out about the DNA match, the Moonlight Strangler called me. He said he wouldn't come after me because I was blood. Well, Cord's his blood, too, and Willie Lee took him hostage and cut him. Have you seen the scars on his chest?"

This wasn't any more comfortable than discussing Willie Lee's serial-killer label. "I'm fine," Cord assured her. "And in that call, the Moonlight Strangler never said he wouldn't come after me."

There was plenty more to this argument, too.

"Besides," Cord went on, "even if your gut won't let you believe Willie Lee is the Moonlight Strangler, then he's still a violent man. And I have the scars to prove it."

He hadn't meant to include that last part. It just flew out of his mouth, and it caused Addie's eyes to fill with yet more concern.

"What if it wasn't Willie Lee who kidnapped you?" Karina suggested. "What if it was someone setting up Willie Lee?"

Again, not a new argument. He could have repeated the facts to her, that there'd been no other DNA or evidence found at the crime scene to indicate Willie Lee had been set up. But Karina was as familiar with the evidence as he was.

Addie reached out, touched his arm and rubbed it gently. Probably trying to soothe that anger inside him. It was a lost cause, but Cord welcomed it anyway.

"Cord told me that Willie Lee worked for you and

your family for a long time," Addie said to Karina. "Would you mind if I asked you some questions about him?"

"I don't mind." But Karina didn't sound so certain of that. Probably because she'd already been grilled six ways to Sunday about the man.

"Was Willie Lee ever mean or violent with you?" Addie continued.

Karina didn't hesitate. "Never. He did punch a man once, but that was to defend my honor." Then, she paused. "Willie Lee became like a father to me after my parents died."

That had Addie tensing a little, and she dropped back a step. "Did he ever say anything about having children?"

"No." Again, no hesitation. Probably because the FBI, and Cord, had asked Karina that multiple times. "But Willie Lee didn't share a lot about himself. Never talked about his past, and whenever it would come up in a general sort of way, he'd get this sad look in his eyes."

Maybe because he'd abandoned his two kids and murdered their mother. But there was enough salt in Karina's wounds without Cord stating the obvious. Still, it could be true. During that phone conversation with Addie, the Moonlight Strangler had told her that he'd killed their mother.

Something that still felt like a cut to the heart.

It didn't matter that Cord couldn't remember any-thing about his mother, the Moonlight Strangler had taken her from Addie and him. And he was going to pay for that.

Cord heard more footsteps, and a moment later Jericho came back in. "Everything okay?" he asked, caution in his voice and expression.

"Fine," Addie assured him. As she'd done with Cord, she went to Jericho and hugged him. "Karina and I were just talking."

Jericho seemed as uncomfortable with that as Cord. But there was something else in Jericho's body language, and since he had stepped out to take the call, maybe there was bad news.

"I'll just be going," Addie said, likely sensing that something was going on. She kissed both Cord and Jericho on their cheeks and added a whispered good-bye. She even gave Karina's hand a gentle squeeze.

Which Cord wished she hadn't done.

He didn't want Karina having any more encouragement for believing Willie Lee was innocent, and even something like a hand squeeze from Addie could do that.

Jericho didn't say anything until Addie was out of the room. "The CSIs found some blood about thirty yards from your barn, where the attack occurred," he explained.

Since the layout of the crime scene was still fresh in his mind, Cord knew that could mean trouble.

"Did you go out there in that area before the ambulance or I got there?" Jericho asked Karina.

"No. Heavens, no. I couldn't even stand up my legs

were so shaky. And Rocky wasn't hurt. I didn't see any injuries on him anyway."

Neither had Cord.

Damn.

This wasn't good because it could mean Rocky was telling the truth about having injured Karina's attacker. Or it could mean he had a partner who had simply gotten hurt in the fray. And if so, there could be at least two thugs out there ready to come after Karina again.

"There's more," Jericho went on. "After I got your text about DeWayne Stringer, I had one of the deputies make some calls. He did indeed have a run-in with Willie Lee, and he apparently isn't a fan of Karina's."

That meshed with what Karina had told him. "Are you bringing him in for questioning?" Cord asked.

Jericho nodded. "He'll be here first thing in the morning." He paused. "Did you know the Comal County sheriff is investigating him?"

"For what?" Karina took the question right out of Cord's mouth.

Jericho drew in a long, frustrated breath. "For murder."

Chapter Six

Karina's eyes flew open, and her heart jolted when she glanced around at the unfamiliar surroundings. She fought through the haze in her mind and the fresh round of panic and remembered where she was.

In Cord's bed.

And she had apparently managed to sleep there, something she hadn't thought possible. Not after the attack and all the other things they'd learned. Still, she'd clearly done more than just take a catnap because the sunlight was peeking through the edge of the blinds.

After they'd left the sheriff's office in the wee hours of the morning, Cord had brought her to his place. Or rather to the guesthouse on the grounds of the Appaloosa Pass Ranch, where he'd been staying since his attack the previous month. His stay there probably wouldn't last much longer, though, because she figured he'd soon be cleared for duty and go back to his apartment in San Antonio.

From the moment Cord had mentioned where he'd

be taking her, she hadn't thought it was a good idea for her to come here.

Karina still didn't.

And now she needed to do something about that and make arrangements for another safe place to stay.

If a safe place was possible, that is.

In addition to Rocky, she had to worry about De-Wayne. Now that Jericho had dropped that bomb-shell about the county sheriff investigating the man.

For murder, no less.

Jericho hadn't gotten all the details, but apparently the county sheriff had found something to make him suspicious of DeWayne, and the sheriff was looking to tie him to the murder of a woman over in Comal County where DeWayne and Karina both lived.

Part of her almost wished that DeWayne had done it. And better yet, that the county sheriff could prove it. That way, DeWayne would be behind bars and not a possible threat to her. Of course, that didn't solve her problem with Rocky unless, during the past hours, Jericho and the deputies had managed to find him.

She got up. Too fast. And had to sit right back down.

That's when she noticed the clothes on the foot of the bed. Jeans, a blue top, some underwear and flip-flops. There was also a handwritten note on top of the neatly folded stack of clothes.

"'Addie sent these over,'" she said, reading the note. "'There are toiletries in the bathroom.'"

Cord had no doubt written the note and left the clothes, but it was a little unnerving to know she'd been so sacked out that she hadn't noticed a man coming into the bedroom. Especially *that* man. It wasn't as if Cord was a wallflower, and he always seemed to get her attention whenever he was around.

Disgusted with that thought, and with herself, Karina forced herself to stand. She scooped up the clothes and went into the adjoining bathroom.

Karina got another jolt, a really bad one, when she caught a glimpse of herself in the mirror and was glad to see that the toiletries mentioned in the note also included some makeup. Including a tube of concealer. She didn't normally wear much makeup, but she would today, though she probably didn't stand much of a chance of covering up the stitches on her cheek or the other bruises.

The one on her forehead was purple.

Since this was the only bathroom in the small guesthouse, she hurried with her shower. She definitely didn't want Cord walking in on her. She hurriedly dressed, too, and even though she did try with the makeup, she finally just gave up. Looking at that god-awful cut on her face turned her stomach, and she already felt lousy enough without seeing it.

Karina made her way to the kitchen. Not that she had to go far. The guesthouse was simply the bedroom suite and an open space area for the kitchen, dining and living room. There were pillows and covers on the sofa, where Cord had spent the night.

Maybe.

But it was just as likely he hadn't slept at all judging from the fatigued look on his face. He was at the window, drinking coffee from a large mug. Since the pot was nearly empty, she figured he'd already had several cups, so she started a fresh pot.

"I need to check on my horses," she said right off the bat.

"Already taken care of. Jericho sent one of the hands over there this morning."

Okay. At least that was one thing she could tick off her list. Still, she'd want to personally check on them soon.

"I'll also want to thank your sister for the clothes," she added. They didn't fit exactly, but it was better than wearing the borrowed scrubs and no underwear.

"Maybe we can stop by your place later so you can get your own things," Cord suggested. "But the CSIs are still out there now so we'll have to wait until they leave."

Of course. And even then Karina wasn't sure she would feel comfortable in the house. And especially not alone. Then again, judging from the *we* that Cord had used, he would be going with her.

"Thank you for putting the clothes in the bedroom," Karina said. "I'm not sure exactly when you did that because I didn't hear you come in."

Not very subtle of her, and he picked up on what she didn't say. "I did knock on the door, but when you didn't answer, I went in to check on you. Just to make sure."

To make sure someone hadn't broken in and tried to murder her again. Karina certainly hadn't forgotten that. Or maybe Cord had just wanted to make sure she hadn't crawled into a corner and gone catatonic.

"Another thanks for doing that," she added. "And for saving my life last night. And for this." She motioned around the guesthouse.

"But?" He stared at her from over the rim of his cup.

For a man he was darn perceptive. She hadn't met many men in her life like that. "*But* I can't stay here. It feels a little like the enemy camp."

"And I'm the enemy." Not exactly a question.

And Karina didn't address it head-on, either. "You don't want me here, and I'm also sure you don't want me in your protective custody any longer than necessary." Too bad she wasn't sure just how much longer that would be.

Cord took his time, had another sip of coffee. "I want you safe, and right now Jericho's got every available deputy tied up with this investigation. I'm on a leave of absence and volunteered to do it."

The corner of her mouth lifted, but it wasn't a smile from humor. "Did Jericho blackmail you or something?"

No mouth lift for him. "It was the only way he would agree to let me be part of the investigation."

Ah. That made sense. No way would Cord want to back away from making sure a copycat had done this. Still, it stung a little. What with arranging for a safe place to stay—and keeping her alive—she had thought maybe he was doing this because…well, it didn't matter what she thought.

She'd been wrong.

"Any breaks in the case?" she asked. Best to keep this conversation professional. Even if he did look hot with his stubble and rumpled hair.

Get a grip.

And some coffee. That might get her mind off Cord. The caffeine might help with the dull throb in her head, too.

Karina went to the counter and poured herself a cup, but she was shaking, and she ended up spilling some of it on her fingers. She barely had time to jerk back her hand and make a small yelp of pain before Cord was there.

He cursed, took the coffee cup from her and pulled her hand beneath the faucet, turning on the cold water. "Just how much are you hurting?"

Now, that was a question she didn't want to answer. And it wasn't just limited to her hand. From the corner of his eye, he glanced at her face. Then, the rest of her body.

Cord looked disgusted with himself again.

"Like you, I'm not hurting at all," she said.

Now, that got a smile tugging at his mouth. She was glad he appreciated her lame attempt at a joke. Glad they could share that smile, too.

Karina was surprised just how much she needed it.

Because while she was indeed hurting in too many places to name, that was only the tip of the iceberg. It felt as if she had a crushing weight on her heart and chest. Her mind, too.

The tears came again, burning her eyes, and she

tried to blink them back. She already felt like a basket case. No sense acting like one.

"Crying's a normal reaction after everything you've been through," Cord said. He kept hold of her hand while the water spilled over it.

"You're not crying," she pointed out, hoping it would get him to smile again. It didn't.

But his gaze did meet hers. "It's a man thing. A couple of my foster fathers taught me that."

That didn't help the crushing feeling in her heart. She'd known Cord had been placed in the system after being abandoned, and unlike his sister, he hadn't been adopted by a loving family. He had been raised in foster care. And not good foster care, from the sound of it.

"I'm sorry you've had such a rough life," she whispered.

Big mistake. He let go of her as if she'd scalded him and took a towel from the drawer so she could dry herself. He would have gone back to the window, but Karina didn't let him get away that easily. She took hold of his arm.

"I shouldn't have brought it up," she told him. "But the apology's still there. I know what it's like to be raised without parents."

Their gazes came together again. And held. Until Cord finally nodded. Maybe that nod was his way of accepting her apology or maybe they had simply reached a truce. Either way, he didn't pull his gaze from her, and she didn't take her hand off him.

There it was.

That tug she felt deep within her belly. And lower. The tug that reminded her of just how attracted she was to him.

He put his hand over hers, keeping it there a moment. Then, two. At first, she thought he might kiss her. Because his attention slid from her eyes to her mouth. That lasted several moments, too.

Before he stepped away from her.

"I can't get involved with you," he said as if that would make this heat all go away. "I can't lose focus. Not while I'm protecting you."

Until he'd added that last part, Karina had thought maybe he was just blowing her off, but that last part made it sound as if one day she might get that kiss after all. Even if it was the last thing she needed from Cord Granger.

He poured her a cup of coffee and went back to his spot at the window. "Talk to me about Mona Wallace," Cord said.

Karina was very familiar with the name, but she hadn't expected Cord to bring up the woman now. "What about her? You know as well as I do that she was murdered and that Willie Lee's DNA was found at the crime scene."

It had been the start of this current nightmare since that DNA meant the cops believed Willie Lee was the Moonlight Strangler.

"Did you know that Mona had a connection to De-Wayne?" he asked.

Karina couldn't shake her head fast enough. "No. I mean, I knew Mona and DeWayne lived in the same

county, but I didn't realize there was a connection."
She froze, and it hit her then. "Does the county sheriff believe DeWayne was the one who killed Mona?"

"He does."

Oh, mercy. This could be the break she'd been looking for. Because if DeWayne had murdered Mona, then it meant DeWayne could have also been the one to plant Willie Lee's DNA at the scene.

"Don't get your hopes up," Cord went on. "The sheriff only has circumstantial evidence. Mona was a married woman, and DeWayne and she had had an affair. But there's no evidence or eyewitnesses to put DeWayne at the crime scene."

It was too late. She had already gotten her hopes up, and Cord had dashed them just as quickly with that reminder.

"Then, why does the county sheriff suspect him?" she asked.

"Because Mona's husband was pushing for DeWayne's arrest. He claims Mona had broken off the affair and that DeWayne was furious, that he'd even threatened her."

Since Karina had been on the receiving end of many of DeWayne's threats, she knew all about his hot temper. "Is there any way to have the evidence from the scene reexamined or—"

"I'm already working on that," Cord interrupted. "I called the FBI this morning to get them started on it. But again, don't get your hopes up. The county CSIs didn't cover that crime scene. The Texas Rangers did, and I'd be surprised if they missed anything."

So would she, but at this point she was simply grasping at straws. If Willie Lee ever came out of that coma, she wanted to be able to tell him that he was a free man. This was the first step in making that happen. Because if DeWayne did kill Mona, then he could have easily planted Willie Lee's DNA at the scene.

Of course, that didn't explain the attack last night.

She was certain, though, that Jericho would ask DeWayne about an alibi when the man came in for questioning. If it was DeWayne, then he would probably find a way to wiggle out of this—alibi included.

"Has Rocky turned up?" she asked. Karina was certain they could get more answers from him, especially after all those photos and news articles that Jax had found in the bunkhouse.

"No sign of him yet. But we did find out that the blood outside the barn isn't the same type as yours. That means it's probably the blood of the person who attacked you, so the lab will put a rush on processing it." He paused. "Now, you *can* get your hopes up about that because both Rocky's and DeWayne's DNA are in the system."

She had to shake her head. "I figured Rocky's would be there because of his record, but DeWayne's, too?"

"He voluntarily gave a sample to the county sheriff when the sheriff started investigating him for murder."

Oh. Karina didn't have to think too long on why he'd agreed to that. DeWayne wouldn't have done it if he'd known there was any chance whatsoever that his DNA would turn up anywhere near Mona's body.

Still, it might be a match to her attacker.

Which brought Karina to her next concern. "That wasn't Rocky talking to us right after the ambulance blew up. I would have recognized his voice."

Cord nodded fast, which meant he'd been thinking about it, too. "Like I said earlier, he could have disguised his voice. Or maybe that was Rocky's partner in crime." He pointed to the laptop on the table.

Karina went closer and saw the webpage for a site called Bloody Murder. Not exactly the sort of site she would surf. Especially since the home page was covered with photos of famous serial killers.

"There are sixty-two members," Cord explained. "They apparently don't consider themselves groupies but rather amateur sleuths. They look through the clues of old cases and try to solve them. Sometimes, they even go so far as to get close to the victim's friends and families."

Sweet heaven. Karina felt violated all over again. Even if Rocky wasn't behind the attack, he'd lied to her, had pretended to be something he wasn't.

"According to their site," Cord went on, "they're convinced Willie Lee is innocent. That he was framed."

She didn't have to think too long about why Cord had mentioned that. "And you believe that's why Rocky attacked me. To make Willie Lee look innocent."

He nodded. "San Antonio PD will be handling this since the club is based there, but they'll take a close look at each member to see if one of them knows where Rocky is. Or if one of them was Rocky's accomplice. I'm betting at least some of them have criminal records, too, so once the CSIs have a DNA profile, they can start comparing it to the club members."

Karina doubted all of that would happen overnight, and that meant she really did have to come up with a different place to stay. However, before she could even bring up the subject, Cord continued.

"I also made a call about Harley Kramer, the guy you had arrested. He's on bail right now, and his trial date is in five days." Cord paused and made eye contact with her again. "And you're the only person scheduled to testify against him."

Karina stopped and gave that some more thought. "At most Harley's only looking at a year or two in jail if he's found guilty. That's not much of a motive for wanting me dead."

"It's a motive, though," Cord concluded. "He's got a very wealthy wife and some in-laws who want all this to go away so he won't muddy their name. And that alone makes him a person of interest in the attack."

Cord didn't add more because his phone rang, and he held it up for her to see.

Jericho's name was on the screen.

When Cord answered it, he put it on speaker, and even though she shouldn't read too much into that, Karina thought maybe he'd done that so she wouldn't go closer to him so she could hear. She definitely got

the feeling that he wanted to keep some distance between them.

"A problem?" Cord asked.

"Maybe," Jericho readily admitted. "DeWayne just
came in, and let's just say, he's not a happy camper.
He's lawyered up already and insists the only person
he'll talk to is Karina. If she's up to it, you should get
her down here right away."

Chapter Seven

Cord wasn't sure Karina was actually *up to* this visit with DeWayne, but she had insisted on coming anyway.

He had to hand it to her. Most people who'd just survived two murder attempts probably wouldn't want to face their possible attacker. But she hadn't backed down an inch.

Maybe not a good thing.

After all, if DeWayne was indeed the one who'd tried to kill her, then it could antagonize the man even more if she went toe-to-toe with him. Still, Cord had no intentions of trying to rein her in. If he'd been in her situation, he would have wanted to do the same thing.

As they'd done the night before, Cord parked his truck in front of the sheriff's offices. Jax had been good enough to bring it to the ranch. Good enough to have been pleasant about dropping it off, too.

Cord's relationship with Addie's adopted brothers wasn't picture-perfect, but since Willie Lee's capture, it'd gotten a little better. At least Cord didn't feel as if they were ready to slug him anytime they saw him. Cord blamed those earlier reactions on his obsession to capture the Moonlight Strangler. An obsession that the Crockett lawmen believed might put Addie in danger.

Thankfully, it hadn't.

Well, not so far anyway.

"Remember, don't let DeWayne get to you," Karina whispered to herself.

Cord figured she'd been giving herself that pep talk since they'd left the ranch. It seemed to be working. She marched into the sheriff's office just ahead of him and made a beeline to the tall, dark-haired man who was standing across from Jericho.

It was DeWayne, all right.

Cord had never met the man, but he had pulled up his DMV photo, and it was a match. However, the photo hadn't shown that smug expression that De-Wayne aimed at Karina. Cord couldn't be sure, but he thought maybe the smugness went up when the man looked at her cuts and bruises.

DeWayne wasn't alone. There was a man about the same age—late fifties—wearing a suit, and he was right by DeWayne's side. His lawyer, no doubt.

"Karina," DeWayne said, smiling. "You came."

Oh, man. With just that handful of words and sick smile, he pissed off Cord. Talk about pompous, and Cord wished he could take him down a notch.

Jericho didn't seem any more pleased with the man than Cord did. "We can take this to the interview room now."

So, DeWayne was waiting on Karina after all. Too bad he hadn't made a confession or two. Of course, his lawyer probably wasn't going to let him say much of anything. That's where some button-pushing came in. Cord was banking on DeWayne's nasty temper that Karina had told him about. If Cord could get the man riled up enough, he might spill all sorts of secrets.

Of course, one of those secrets could topple the case against Willie Lee. But that was a bridge Cord would cross if he came to it.

"I have an alibi for last night," DeWayne said without any prompting. He strolled into the interview room, hands stuffed into the pockets of his overpriced designer jeans, and he sank down into one of the chairs.

Cord looked at Jericho to see if he knew anything about that so-called alibi. "He says he was with a friend. I'm having Levi check it out now."

"Oh, I was with her, all right," DeWayne insisted. "And I didn't leave her place until this morning. She'll vouch for me."

"Or lie for you," Cord said. He couldn't help himself.

No flash of temper, but DeWayne did turn that sickening smile on Karina. "Of course, my lawyer could have handled all these false accusations that you're making, but I wanted to see you. Did you do something different with your hair?" And he laughed.

Cord was certain he had his own flash of temper.

Karina, however, hardly reacted. Which meant

she'd likely been on the receiving end of this idiot's bull way too often.

"I'd like to talk about Mona," Karina said, her voice as calm as she was trying to look.

That's when Cord realized she had her hands clenched into fists and that her knuckles were turning white. He ushered her to the chair across the table from DeWayne and had her sit down. At least that way DeWayne couldn't see her hands and the effect he was having on her.

But Karina also had an effect on DeWayne.

"Mona," DeWayne repeated, his eyes narrowing for just a split second. "What about her?"

"Did you kill her?" Cord asked.

That had an effect, too. Cord got a dose of those narrowed eyes. Maybe DeWayne hadn't thought they would discuss the woman, that this chat would be solely about alibis and attacks. But DeWayne was wrong.

The narrowed eyes went away, but DeWayne huffed, the sort of huff a man might make if he was bored with the subject. "You've been talking to Sheriff Ezell over in Comal County. Wouldn't put much stock into what he's saying. He's basing everything on what he heard from a jealous man."

"Mona's husband," Cord said. "The sheriff doesn't think it's just the jealousy talking."

"Well, he's wrong." Now, there was some temper. A tightening of the mouth. The sharp tone. There was just a glimpse of it before he pulled back his claws. "I've already admitted to having an affair with Mona.

Plenty of men had affairs with her. I hope you and the sheriff are pestering them as much as you're pestering me."

Karina rolled her eyes. "If you're just going to rehash what we already know, then why ask me to come here?"

Cord figured DeWayne would dole out another smart-mouthed answer, but he didn't. He sat there, his face muscles stirring, before he looked at Karina again.

"Because I don't want you thinking I did this to you," DeWayne finally said. But he said it through clenched teeth. "I have enough legal battles dealing with Sheriff Ezell without you adding this to it. The man's like a dog with a bone. He won't let go of this Mona thing."

Cord liked the sheriff already, and he hadn't even met him. "I guess you have something to convince us that you didn't attack Karina?" he said to DeWayne.

"Maybe. Someone broke into my house a few days ago. I thought it was a kid since they didn't take anything, but then I had a PI look at the security feed. He managed to ID the intruder. A guy named Scott Chaplin. He belongs to some stupid club called Bloody Murder."

Well, that got Cord's attention. "Have you spoken to this guy?"

DeWayne shook his head. "My PIs haven't been able to find him, but I found out a lot about him. The club is a group of losers trying to prove Willie Lee isn't the Moonlight Strangler." He paused. "I'm worried that he might have planted some kind of evidence in my house."

"Evidence?" Jericho challenged.

DeWayne reached into his shirt pocket. And Cord automatically slid his hand over his gun. Jericho would have searched DeWayne when he first came in and disarmed him if necessary, but Cord didn't want to take any chances that the guy might have sneaked in a knife.

However, it wasn't a weapon that DeWayne pulled out. It was a small plastic bag containing what appeared to be a note.

"I found this on the desk in my home office." DeWayne put the bag on the table, and Karina, Jericho and Cord had a closer look.

"'You'll pay for planting that DNA at the crime scene,'" Jericho said, reading aloud. He huffed and looked at DeWayne. "Please tell me you gave this to Sheriff Ezell."

Judging from DeWayne's scowl, the answer to that was no. "He's already trying to railroad me for murder. This wouldn't have helped."

"And it won't help now," Cord assured him. Which brought him to his next question. "Why bring it to us?"

DeWayne stayed quiet a moment. "Because I thought it would convince you that I'm in danger, too. That I'm not the one after Karina. I think we're both in danger from the idiots in that club."

Karina leaned in, staring at DeWayne. "I didn't set up Willie Lee," she said.

"Neither did I!" DeWayne snapped. "But these dimwits think I did. Hell, like I said, they could have planted something in my house."

"Like what?" Cord pressed.

"I don't know," DeWayne shouted, but he stopped, paused, regrouped. "Something to do with Mona maybe. They could have perhaps stolen some evidence. And Sheriff Ezell might have stood back and watched them do it. Anyway, I figure the same person after Karina is after me, too."

His concern seemed genuine. *Seemed.* But Cord wasn't about to buy in to this. Judging from Jericho's huff, neither was he.

"I'll have the note sent to the lab so it can be checked for prints and trace," Jericho said. "I'll also want that security footage of this Scott Chaplin guy in your house. But I'm keeping Sheriff Ezell in the loop. Save your breath and don't bother to argue about that. I'll call you when and if I want to talk to you again. In the meantime, you stay away from Karina."

Jericho picked up the note and started out of the room.

"That's it?" DeWayne practically jumped to his feet. "You're not going to arrest every single member in that stupid club right now?"

"No," Jericho said from over his shoulder as he walked away.

DeWayne's temper flared again, and his face was turning red when he shifted his attention to Karina. "You believe me, don't you?"

"You've never cared what I thought of you before," she growled.

DeWayne pointed his finger at her. "I won't let you and these local yokels try to pin this on me. If I'd wanted you dead, you would be."

Oh, hell. That was the wrong thing to say, and Cord felt himself moving before he even knew he was going to do it. He got right in DeWayne's face.

"Is that a threat?" Cord didn't wait for him to answer. "Because as a local yokel, it sounded like a threat to me."

DeWayne looked plenty ready to return verbal fire, but the sound of voices stopped him. Jericho's was one of those voices, but Cord didn't recognize the man Jericho seemed to be arguing with.

But Karina and DeWayne appeared to know who it was.

Karina got to her feet, and both DeWayne and she left the room and went into the hall. Cord didn't think it was his imagination that Karina suddenly looked less steady than she had just seconds earlier.

Their visitor was likely the reason for that.

While Cord hadn't recognized his voice, it was a face he recognized because he'd checked out all their suspects' driver's license photos. And this was definitely one of their suspects.

Harley Kramer.

No visible weapon. Harley had just a phone in his hand.

One thing was for sure—Karina was right about the scars. Very noticeable. But he didn't look like a

B and E suspect. He was wearing a suit. A nice one, too. Probably the result of his wife's money. However, a suit couldn't smooth away his craggy face and the lines around his eyes. Harley looked every one of his fifty-nine years and then some.

"You weren't supposed to be here for another hour," Jericho said, checking the time.

"I came early. Good thing, too." His attention zoomed right to Karina. Then, to DeWayne. Judging from the glare he gave DeWayne, Harley wasn't a fan, either. "Because I'm betting that SOB is telling lies about me."

"I didn't mention you," DeWayne fired back.

"How do these two know each other?" Cord asked Karina.

"Harley came to me and accused me of setting up Willie Lee," DeWayne snarled. "I'd never even met this joker, and he starts spreading lies about me. About how I want to get back at Willie Lee and Karina."

"I don't have a beef with you," Harley argued. "Other than I want you to tell the truth. I know Willie Lee, and he's not a killer."

Apparently, Willie Lee had someone else in his corner. Interesting. But then again, Harley had already admitted that he knew Willie Lee. Cord would press him about that first chance he got.

"I want Harley arrested," DeWayne went on. "I want him grilled like you just grilled me."

"That wasn't a grilling," Cord assured him. "When it happens, you'll know."

That put some fire in DeWayne's eyes. Enough fire that his lawyer noticed and took his client by the arm. "We should be going," DeWayne's attorney said to him.

Cord agreed with the lawyer. He needed some time to check out whatever was going on between Harley and DeWayne. Needed to find Scott Chaplin, too. First, though, he had to finish up here so he could get Karina far away from both of these clowns. She was trembling again, and that steel she'd fought so hard to maintain in the interview room was melting away fast.

"Leave," Jericho told DeWayne when he just stood there and glared at Harley. "Unless you'd rather I put you in a holding cell for forty-eight hours?"

DeWayne turned his glare on Jericho. Then, on Karina and Cord before he stormed out with his lawyer.

Harley kept his attention on the man until he got into his car and drove off. Only then did Harley open his mouth to continue, but Jericho stopped that by frisking him. Even though Harley had to know it was standard procedure for anyone entering the sheriff's office, he still managed to look insulted.

"I'm here to help you," Harley snarled at Karina. "But you treat me like a criminal."

"Help me?" Karina questioned. "And how exactly do you want to do that?"

"By giving you information that could save your life." He made an uneasy glance over his shoulder.

Cord hated to look a gift horse in the mouth, but

he wasn't sure he could trust anything Harley gave them. He also hated those glances that the man kept making. It was as if he was waiting for a killer to jump out at him.

"Before we continue this little chat," Jericho interrupted, "tell me where you were last night."

Harley huffed, no doubt because he thought he was still being treated unfairly. The treatment wouldn't get any better unless he had an alibi.

"I was at my house in San Antonio, and I was alone all night because my wife's out of town. I thought it might be a good time for her to take a long trip to Europe." Harley cursed. "If I'd known I was going to need an alibi, I would have gone out with friends or something. But that doesn't make me guilty of hurting Karina. It just makes me a loner."

Maybe it made him a would-be killer, too.

"Did you make any calls while you were home?" Jericho persisted.

Harley paused as if giving that some thought and shook his head. "No."

"Well, then, it won't take long to go through your phone records." Jericho motioned for Harley to hand him the phone.

"I'll give it to you in a minute," Harley said. "First, though, I have to show Karina a picture I took. I think it's the guy who tried to hurt her last night."

She didn't react to it as if it was a bombshell. Probably because she didn't trust or believe Harley, either. But Harley seemed convinced he had something.

"I need to tell you about him first," Harley explained, looking not at Karina but Cord then Jericho. "Because I don't want you two arresting me or anything."

"Do we have reason to arrest you?" Cord challenged.

That put some anger in his eyes, and he turned to Karina to continue. "I stumbled onto this by accident when I was at a bar in San Antonio the night before last. I heard two guys talking. Nut jobs. They were saying how they thought the cops had framed Willie Lee and that they should do something about it."

"Do what exactly?" Karina asked when Harley didn't continue.

Harley shook his head and took a deep breath. "Kill somebody and make it look like the Moonlight Strangler."

Everything inside Cord went on alert. Because if this was true, then Harley had been in the right place at exactly the right time to hear just what they needed to hear to solve this.

Well, maybe.

If Harley had been the one to attack Karina, he could be using this as a way to deflect the guilt off him. It wouldn't work unless there was a whole lot of evidence to back it up.

"Did you get their names?" Cord asked.

"No. I didn't exactly feel good about going to two morons who were just talking about murder." Harley held up his phone again. "But I took their picture."

All right. So maybe that was evidence.

"Any reason you didn't tell us about this two nights

ago?" Jericho demanded before he even looked at the photo.

"I thought…hoped that it was just talk. And then I heard about the attack and knew they'd done it."

Cord snatched the phone from Harley then, and he expected to see an out-of-focus shot. It wasn't. The image was crystal clear.

Clear enough to cause Karina to gasp.

Because the man in the picture was someone they both recognized.

Chapter Eight

Rocky.

Karina knew she shouldn't be shocked at seeing his picture on Harley's phone, but it still hit her hard. For days, Rocky had been right by her side, helping her with the horses, and all that time he'd wanted her dead.

If Harley was telling the truth, that is.

She reminded herself that Harley did indeed hate her, and he could want her out of the way so she couldn't testify against him at his trial. Somehow, that was easier to accept than Rocky choosing her as some random victim to copycat the Moonlight Strangler.

"We need to find Rocky," she said under her breath.

Until she heard her own words spoken aloud, Karina hadn't realized just how shaky she was. But Cord must have because he took hold of her arm and led her back toward Jericho's office.

"That's it?" Harley called out to her. "I give you picture proof, and you just walk away?"

Karina stopped. "Thank you," she managed to say, but it was hollow. Maybe not even deserved. Harley could be playing some kind of sick game with her. "But you broke into Willie Lee's cabin. Someone who does that isn't exactly trustworthy."

"Willie Lee would want me to have those pictures," Harley insisted. Something he'd said, and repeated, right from the start.

And he didn't stop there.

"Just pictures," he added. "I wasn't after anything of value. I only wanted mementos from an old friend. And now I'm facing charges for that. Any idea what this is doing to my wife and her family?"

She nodded. Karina did know. Harley's wife, Miriam, was a socialite. An apparently beloved one. And people had praised her for marrying a disfigured man. Well, Karina wasn't going to let Harley's wife, or his scars, keep her from getting to the truth.

Harley demanded that she come back and talk to him face-to-face and was still essentially calling her out when Cord and she went into the office. Cord shut the door, and Harley instantly went quiet. It was possible Jericho had threatened the man, or perhaps it wasn't any fun to torment her if she wasn't around to listen.

"I don't even know what Harley was really looking for in Willie Lee's cabin," she admitted. "And yes, I searched the place. No pictures. I'm talking zero. In fact, Willie Lee had nothing personal in there."

That had to interest a lawman, and Cord no doubt believed that meant Willie Lee was leading some kind of secret life.

The life of a serial killer.

"Let's assume for a second that Harley was indeed an old friend," Cord mused. "Maybe he's looking for something Willie Lee hid away. Nothing to do with the Moonlight Strangler," Cord quickly added when she opened her mouth to object. "But maybe they committed some other crime. Something that Harley wanted to make sure didn't come back to bite him."

"Like what?" she asked, caution in her voice.

Cord lifted his shoulder. "There was a big money-laundering operation going on at the time the murders started over thirty years ago. Willie Lee and Harley would have been in their midtwenties then. Someone died as a result of that operation. Again, I'm not saying that Willie Lee did it, but there's no statute of limitations on murder. That would be a good reason for Harley to break into the cabin."

It would be. And she wasn't naive enough to believe Willie Lee had a perfect past. Still, it was hard to think of him as a criminal. Any kind of criminal.

"We'll leave as soon as Harley's out of here," Cord added, checking his watch. "I just want to make sure neither he nor DeWayne follows us."

Mercy, she hadn't even thought of that, but she wouldn't put it past either of them. Plus, she wasn't exactly thrilled with the idea of going back to the Appaloosa Pass Ranch.

Cord went to Jericho's computer, and after he pulled up the results of his search, he showed it to her. "That's Scott Chaplin's DMV photo. Do you recognize him?"

Karina shook her head. That was something at

least. She wasn't sure she could have stomached knowing that both Rocky and Scott had somehow insinuated themselves into her life.

She leaned against the back of the door, looked at Cord and saw something she didn't usually see in his eyes. Sympathy. As someone who'd always had to stand on her own two feet, it stung to have someone feel sorry for her.

Karina tried to put on a much stronger face. "I need a place to stay. And it's not as if I have a lot of options. I'm guessing my ranch in Comal County is out." She didn't wait for Cord to confirm that.

It was out.

All three of their suspects would look for her there. And besides, going there could endanger the six ranch hands who worked for her. No way did she want to bring this to their doorstep.

"I'm not exactly close to my friends these days," she went on. "Because of Willie Lee. They think I'm crazy to believe he's innocent."

And mercy, could she sound any more miserable?

She wouldn't have been surprised if Cord had just groaned and walked out. But he didn't. He just stood there, staring at her, as if he was waiting for her to quit whining and do something.

So she did do something.

Karina kissed him.

It was barely a brush of her mouth to his, but she still felt it in every inch of her. She snapped away from him, ready to apologize and promise that it wouldn't happen again. But the words died on her lips when Cord slid his hand around the back of her neck.

"If we're going to make a mistake, it might as well be a good one," he drawled.

And he kissed her.

Not some brief little peck, either. This was a real kiss, and Karina could have sworn she lost every bit of her breath. It just vanished, and for those moments he was kissing her, all the pain and the flashbacks vanished, too.

She heard herself make a sound, a mixture of relief and pleasure. Mostly pleasure. From practically the moment Karina had first laid eyes on Cord, she'd wondered what it would be like to kiss him.

And now she knew.

He eased back from her, slowly, meeting her eye to eye. "Was that a big enough mistake for you?"

She couldn't help it. Karina smiled.

Cord didn't smile, though. He apparently wasn't feeling any relief, but she was certain that she saw the heat in his eyes that was mirrored in her own. He stepped away, turning his back to her for a moment as if he was trying to regain control. Or maybe he was just cursing himself for that lapse in judgment.

"I need you to stay at the Appaloosa Pass Ranch just one more day," he said.

Karina hadn't been sure what he was about to tell her, but she certainly hadn't expected that. And then something occurred to her.

"You didn't kiss me just so I'd cooperate with you, did you?" she asked.

He angled his head, looking back at her, and she had her answer with just that one glance.

No.

That wasn't the reason he'd kissed her.

Well, good. Her state of mind was already eggshell-thin, and she didn't want another hit. Especially since she wasn't so sure that kiss was indeed a mistake.

"The Appaloosa Pass Ranch has security already in place," Cord said a few seconds later. "A day will give Jericho and his deputies time to find Rocky, and it'll give me time to figure out where to take you."

"I'm staying in your protective custody?" she asked. Karina hadn't added *after that kiss*, but she figured Cord understood the full question.

"Yeah. For the time being anyway. I'll work on that, too."

But he might not be able to get everything in place in twenty-four hours. And Jericho certainly might not be able to find Rocky by then.

"I need some things at my rental house. Clothes, for one thing," she said, motioning toward the borrowed items Addie had lent her. "Plus, I take meds for my thyroid. When will I be able to get back into the house to get those things?"

Cord took out his phone, sent a text and thankfully got a response almost right away. "Jax said you can stop by now," he answered after reading the text. "The CSIs are still there, but they can escort us in and out."

He got her moving out of the office, and Karina braced herself for another round with Harley.

"He's gone," Jericho volunteered. "I had nothing I could use to hold him."

Karina had been afraid of that. Yes, Harley hadn't shown them that picture sooner, but it would be hard to pin withholding-evidence charges on him when they weren't even sure Rocky was the one who'd tried to kill her.

"But I did just get an interesting phone call," Jericho added. "A woman named Taryn Wellman."

"I know her. She's DeWayne's current girlfriend." Karina had to shake her head. "But why would she call you?"

"Because she's apparently worried about lover boy. She says he's been acting suspicious and that she's afraid someone's blackmailing him or something."

"Blackmail?" Cord questioned.

"She didn't have a lick of proof. No other details, either. Hell, maybe because there aren't any details to have. I'll check it out, of course, but DeWayne could just be fooling around with another woman, that's all."

Yes. That sounded like DeWayne. According to the rumor mill, he'd had several lovers in the short time since he'd moved near her, one during the same time as Taryn.

"I'm taking Karina to her place and then back to the ranch," Cord told Jericho. "I'll work from there with the SAPD on contacting the members of the Bloody Murder club. One of them has to know where Rocky is."

Jericho nodded, and Cord and she headed out toward his truck. As he'd done earlier, he got her inside fast, and they sped away from the sheriff's office. Karina glanced around to make sure no one was following them. Cord did the same.

"I've been thinking about Harley just showing up at your ranch," Cord said. "Jericho and I discussed it earlier, but I forgot to ask Harley about this particular point. Did Harley happen to tell you how he knew Willie Lee and your mother?"

It took her a moment to switch mental gears. Partly because her mind was still hazy from that kiss. And also because there seemed to be some kind of accusation in his tone. Probably because she'd said Harley gave her the creeps.

"Harley was short on specifics, but he said Willie Lee and he were old army buddies." She paused. "And that he'd met my mother after my father died."

Cord didn't say anything. Probably because he was waiting for more. But Karina figured this wasn't going to make sense to him.

"I don't know if my mother and Harley actually met," she went on. "I certainly never saw him around the ranch. But my mother suffered from depression, and Harley knew all about that. He said he was trying to help her, but that clearly didn't work. She finally overdosed on pills one night."

Of course, Harley could have gotten those details from the same gossip mill where she'd gotten dirt about DeWayne's affair.

"Did Harley talk to you about your mother's suicide?" Cord asked.

Karina had to shake her head. "No, only that he knew my mother was dead and that he was sorry about that because he loved her."

And she could say the same for herself. Karina had indeed loved her mother. Once. But after the woman had fallen apart and quit living, she had become a hard woman to love.

There was a lesson in that for Karina.

She couldn't let all of what happened break her. She had to keep fighting, not only to find the person who'd attacked her, but also to figure out a way to prove Willie Lee's innocence.

Cord didn't ask her anything else. He drove in silence, but it wasn't a peaceful drive. He kept watch all around them, and he didn't seem to relax one bit when he finally pulled up in front of her rental place. But then neither did she.

There was yellow crime-scene tape on the barn and the area around it, and a CSI van was parked next to the house. Both reminders of the attack.

"Let's make this fast," he insisted. Cord reached to open his door, but then stopped. He stopped her, too.

Karina wasn't sure why he'd done that, but she followed his gaze. He was looking at the barn, specifically at the opened door, where the wind was rattling the yellow tape.

"What's wrong?" she asked.

He only shook his head and kept his attention pinned there.

She wasn't touching Cord, but Karina knew the exact moment that his muscles tightened. And he pulled his gun.

That put her heart in her throat, and she was about to ask him again what was going on. But she saw it for herself.

Someone was moving inside the barn.

"It's probably one of the CSIs," she said, hoping that was true.

It wasn't.

The person moved again, and for just a split second, Karina got a good look at him.

It was Rocky.

CORD COULDN'T TELL if Rocky had a gun, but he couldn't risk it. Nor could he take the chance of having Karina run into the house with the CSIs.

"Get down on the seat," Cord told Karina, and he threw open the door.

"You can't go out there." She caught on to his arm.

Cord shook off her grip and maneuvered himself into a position to take aim while still using the door as cover. Not that it would be much cover if Rocky did indeed have a weapon, but it was better than nothing.

He tossed Karina his phone. "Text Jax and tell him what's going on. I don't want the CSIs walking out of the house and getting caught in gunfire. I also want somebody out here to take Rocky into custody." Cord didn't want to do that himself, not with Karina with him.

She nodded, and despite the fact that Karina had to be shaken up by this, she got busy with the text. And Cord got busy with their suspect.

"Rocky?" Cord called out. "I need you to come out of the barn with your hands up."

No answer.

Damn.

Cord was hoping Rocky would make this easy. But apparently no such luck.

"We know about the Bloody Murder club," Cord tried again. "We also know you discussed a copycat killing so you could clear Willie Lee. I'm not just going to let you walk away from this."

Especially since he could return to have another go at Karina.

If that's what he'd done.

The seconds crawled by and Cord glanced at the house when he saw some movement there. One of the CSIs was looking out the window. He didn't recognize the guy, but he had his creds clipped to his shirt pocket. Cord motioned for him to move back. The county CSIs weren't issued guns as part of their jobs, but many carried their personal weapons. He hoped that was the case here because he might need backup before this was over.

Thankfully, Cord could see both of the barn doors, so it would be easy to spot Rocky if he tried to escape. However, there were trees, fences and watering troughs nearby. Plenty of places for someone to hide and wait for an ambush. That was even more reason to hurry this along.

"Rocky, get out here now!" Cord shouted, though he didn't hold out much hope the man would answer. That's why Cord was so surprised when he did.

"I can't do this," Rocky said. Not a shout like Cord's. He seemed to be arguing with someone. Or maybe himself.

"Yes, you can come out," Cord insisted. "Because if you don't, I have to come in there after you."

It wasn't a bluff. Not exactly. Eventually, Cord would have to go inside the barn, but that wouldn't happen until he had backup in place and someone to help him protect Karina.

"I need to end this," Rocky added. Cord couldn't be sure, but it sounded as if he was crying. Or else pretending to cry.

"Maybe I should try?" Karina asked. "I might be able to talk him into surrendering."

Cord was about to tell her no, that he wanted her down on the seat. However, before he could even get out a single word, there was a sound. A really bad one.

A shot blasted through the air.

And it was quickly followed by another one. Both bullets slammed into the bed of his truck, just inches from where Cord was standing.

Cord jumped back in the truck, slamming the door and trying to position himself in front of Karina. The sides of the truck were reinforced—a modification he'd made after being attacked by the Moonlight Strangler—but the bullets could still tear their way through.

"Backup will be here soon," she told him.

That was good, but soon might not be soon enough, though.

The bullets just kept coming, and Cord tried to pinpoint Rocky's position. But the shots weren't coming from the barn. They were coming from the direction of the bunkhouse.

Hell.

Rocky wasn't alone.

"It's Scott Chaplin," Karina said. "I recognize him from the photo you showed me."

And that's when Cord realized she was peering over the dash and at the doorway of the bunkhouse, where the man was standing. Cord pushed her back down on the seat and hoped she would stay put so he could figure out what the devil was going on.

He looked at the man again. Yeah, it was Scott.

But something wasn't right.

Cord didn't actually see a gun in Scott's hand, and the man darted out of sight before he could get a better look. He couldn't see Rocky any longer, either.

However, the shots continued.

All coming from the side of the bunkhouse. Did that mean Scott and Rocky had brought another member of the group with them?

The CSI that Cord had spotted from the window opened the front door of the house. He was armed, and even though he took aim in the direction of the bunkhouse, he didn't fire. Probably because he didn't know if this was a hostage situation or not.

Cord didn't know, either.

But he had to put a stop to the shooter. Cord hit the button to lower the window, and he levered himself up so he could get the guy in his sights.

And Cord fired.

The shooter scrambled back, but Cord sent another shot his way. Then, a third.

With the sounds of the blasts still ringing in his ears, it took Cord a moment to hear the other sounds. An ax or something striking against the wood in the barn.

Great. Now, Rocky could be trying to escape.

"Cover me," Cord called out to the CSI who had now made his way onto the porch. He took a backup gun from the glove compartment and handed it to Karina. "Stay down but try to keep your eye on him."

"On the CSI?" she asked, her eyes widening.

"Yeah." Cord hated that he'd just caused her fear to soar even higher, but he didn't know the CSI and wasn't ready to completely trust him with his and Karina's lives.

Cord climbed over her and got out through the passenger's door so he could hurry to the rear of his truck. The CSI reacted, too, moving to the end of the porch and aiming his gun at the bunkhouse.

The sounds of the chopping continued. And it was coming from the side nearest the truck.

What the hell was Rocky thinking?

Cord would still be able to gun him down, but if he did that, the man wouldn't be able to give them answers. Cord preferred that not to happen.

Another shot came from the bunkhouse. This one was aimed at the CSI. The CSI dropped back a step, using the house for cover, but he didn't stay there. The CSI fired into the bunkhouse.

And this time, he hit something.

Or rather someone.

Scott came staggering out the front door. He was clutching his chest, and there was blood all over his shirt. He said something, or rather he tried, but Cord didn't catch a word of it before Scott collapsed onto the ground.

"No!" Rocky yelled.

Repeating that shout, Rocky tore through the rest of the wood and crawled out. He dropped onto his knees, his attention staying on Scott. That's when Cord spotted the gun in Rocky's right hand. His phone was in his left.

"Don't die. Don't be dead," Rocky said. He tossed both the gun and phone at Cord, got to his feet and started running.

But so did Cord.

He hurried toward Rocky, blocking his path and pointing his gun right in the man's face.

"Move one inch," Cord warned Rocky, "and you're a dead man."

Chapter Nine

Karina knew she couldn't ever come back to this place. The attack on her alone would have made her feel that way, but now she was certain of it. There'd been more blood spilled.

And there was a dead man lying in front of the bunkhouse.

The CSI had confirmed that fact not long after he'd shot him and while Cord was putting a pair of plastic cuffs on Rocky. Rocky wasn't looking at Cord, her or the body. He was staring blankly at the ground. Probably because he'd just seen his friend and fellow club member die right in front of him.

"You should stay in the truck a while longer," the CSI said, making his way toward her.

According to his name tag, he was Mitchell Durst, and the woman who had come out of the house shortly afterward was Helen Krauss, another CSI. Even though they both often dealt with violent crime scenes, they were visibly shaken.

Karina was, as well.

Before Cord had even gotten out of the truck, he'd

given her a gun and told her to keep an eye on the CSI. Karina still had the gun gripped in her hand, but she was fairly sure the CSI wasn't a threat. However, it suddenly felt as if anyone and anything could be.

All except Cord.

He'd saved her life, again.

Karina heard the sirens on the cruisers long before they pulled into her driveway. Jax and the other deputy, Dexter, got out of the first cruiser. Jax hurried toward Cord, while Dexter headed for the dead body.

Scott Chaplin.

Karina wanted to believe this was the end of it now that Scott was dead and Rocky was in custody, but there were other club members out there.

And so was the real Moonlight Strangler.

She wasn't safe, and thanks to her getting Cord involved, neither was he. Any one of those bullets could have killed him.

Jax took over with Rocky, and the two deputies who pulled up in the other cruiser went to help Jax with the arrest. Cord kicked aside Rocky's gun, probably so that it would be well out of the man's reach, and he picked up Rocky's phone. Cord looked at her, but he had a short conversation with Jax and then made a call with his own phone before he started toward her.

"The horses are all okay," Cord said. "Jericho's hand had moved them to the back pasture early this morning. Neither the ranch hand nor the horses were anywhere near those shots."

In the grand scheme of things, most people might

not have considered it important for her to know that. But it was.

"Thank you for checking," she said, finally managing to get out the words. "Did Rocky say anything about why he was here?"

Cord shook his head and opened the door to help her out. "But he probably realized he was in a lot of trouble and needed a lawyer before he started talking. We can wait inside until the scene's cleared enough for us to leave."

He didn't say how long that would be, and Karina wasn't sure she wanted to hear the answer anyway.

While Cord led her up the porch, she glanced back at Rocky. The deputies were hauling him to the second cruiser. No doubt taking him to the sheriff's office so he could be jailed. Jax joined Dexter by the body.

Both of the CSIs were outside, so that's probably why Cord locked the door. However, it was a reminder that there could be others out there. Not exactly a thought to steady her nerves.

"Go ahead and gather up the things you wanted to get," Cord added. "That way, when Jax gives us the green light, we can leave right away."

Good. Even though the alternative wasn't much better.

"What if someone comes after me at the Appaloosa Pass Ranch?" she asked, going straight to her bedroom.

Cord followed her but didn't answer until she looked back at him. "I can't give guarantees this won't happen again. Hell, it happened right under my nose. But I can make the guesthouse at the ranch as safe as I can make any place."

Which wasn't 100 percent. Nothing was at this point.

Since she felt she had to keep moving or else she would collapse, Karina went to the closet, took out a suitcase and started shoving clothes into it. She knew she was moving too fast, that she probably looked like a malfunctioning windup toy, but she couldn't stop herself.

She hurried to the dresser and grabbed some underwear, tossing them into the suitcase, too. Karina would have done the same to her toiletries in the bathroom, but Cord took her by the hand to stop her in her tracks.

"I'm not going to cry," she insisted. "I can be as strong as you."

"You already are."

Damn him. It was the right thing to say. Perfect, in fact. And that's why she didn't listen to her common sense and back away from him when he pulled her into his arms. Besides, she wanted to be in his arms. Being there took the edge off the nerves, and it got her mind off the fact that she'd just seen a man die.

"Most people have a meltdown, a major one, when violence happens around them," Cord went on. His voice was as soothing as his arms.

"The meltdown still might happen," Karina mumbled. "Especially when I run out of things to pack."

She certainly hadn't meant to make that sound like

a joke, but Cord smiled. It was lazy and slow like the long look he gave her before he lowered his head and did something she hadn't seen coming.

He kissed her.

Judging from the soft sound he made, he wasn't sure who was more surprised by that—him or her. Karina was thinking he'd won on that count. She'd dreamed of doing this since that kiss in Jericho's office, but she was betting Cord had been spending his mental energy on making sure it didn't happen again.

But here it was. Another kiss. And it was a good one.

Being in his arms had been incredible, but this took things up a mile-high notch. How could someone taste that good? And make her forget, for a few seconds anyway, about the nightmare that'd just happened.

Karina got lost in the kiss. Cord did, too. And while she figured he hadn't wanted this to go much further, it did. He lowered his hands to her waist, pulling her closer. And closer. Until they were plastered right against each other.

Mercy.

It'd been a long time since she'd felt this kind of fire. And never like this. Karina found herself wanting more, and she was the one who deepened the kiss. The one who pulled him even closer. Until she couldn't breathe. Couldn't think.

But Cord could apparently hear, because he stopped.

"My phone," he said, breaking away from her and taking out his cell.

Great day. She hadn't even heard the ringing sound,

but sure enough it was Jax. No doubt important. And she'd been so lost in that kiss, she hadn't even heard it. So much for the vigilance she needed to make sure they weren't attacked again.

"You still got Rocky's phone?" Jax asked when Cord answered the call and put it on speaker.

"Yeah. You need it?"

"Not yet, but if what he says is true, I will. Rocky claims he's been getting texts from the Moonlight Strangler. Check and see if there are any messages from God. And yeah, you heard that right."

Cord scowled, maybe at the name or maybe because he thought this was part of the game that Rocky and his club buddies were playing. He took out Rocky's phone, scrolled through the messages and then stopped.

"God," Cord repeated, "texted Rocky three times, and Rocky answered two of them."

Jax cursed. "Is there anything in the messages that jumps out at you?"

"Not really." He glanced through all the messages. "But they need to be analyzed, of course. There might be something important in them." He didn't sound very hopeful, though. "Did Rocky say anything else?" Cord asked. "Like maybe something about there being a third shooter?"

Karina's stomach dropped. A third one? Good grief, how many people wanted her dead?

"Rocky didn't mention anything about a third guy, but he said he's innocent. And that Scott was, too."

Of course, he would say that. "Then why was he here with a gun?" Karina asked. "And why didn't he just turn himself in to the cops?"

"He claims he wanted to get his stuff. By that, I'm guessing he wanted all those photos and newspaper clippings. You know, the very things that will incriminate him when he's arrested?"

"He was trying to cover his tracks," Cord said as if giving that some thought. "But it was pretty gutsy of him and his buddies to come here with the CSIs still around."

Jax made a sound to indicate he was giving it some thought, too. "It doesn't add up. He's hiding something. Or maybe he thought he could hide out until he got another shot at Karina."

The chill came so fast that Karina had to fight off a shudder. Had that been it? Had Rocky been waiting to kill her?

"Jericho will grill him during interrogation," Jax added. "Dexter and the other deputy, Mack, are taking Rocky to the sheriff's office now. Once the ME gets here, I can follow Karina and you back, too, so you can listen to what Rocky has to say."

That meant she wouldn't be going to the ranch. Not right away. It also meant she'd have to give yet another statement of yet another attack. Her third one in less than twenty-four hours.

Cord ended the call and sank down on the foot of her bed. His attention went straight back to Rocky's phone, and she sat down next to him so she could go through the messages with him.

There were five in total—three from "God" and two responses from Rocky. The first was by far the longest, and it had been sent nearly five weeks earlier, right before Willie Lee had been captured. Karina read it word for word.

"'I saw your website, and I thought you might like to chat with me instead of just collecting pictures and doing all that blogging. I'm the Moonlight Strangler, aka the object of your affection. Since you seem like the sort who needs proof that I'm really him, here you go—I took a necklace from Gracie Hernandez. The cops didn't put that in the reports, but if you dig, you'll find out it's true. Bye for now.'"

She looked at Cord, and he nodded. "The Moonlight Strangler did take the woman's necklace. She was photographed wearing it just an hour or so before she was murdered, and it wasn't on her body when the cops found her. Her family said she never took the necklace off."

That twisted at her stomach, but Karina reminded herself that someone in law enforcement could have leaked the info. Still, why go to the trouble of pretending to be the Moonlight Strangler? It wasn't a smart thing to do since the serial killer had gone after those impersonating him.

"Here's Rocky's response," Cord continued. According to the time, he'd sent the text later that same day.

"'I can't confirm about the necklace, the cops won't talk to me, but I do believe you're the Moonlight Strangler. Can you *please* call me?'" *Please* was all in caps and underlined.

It sickened Karina to think that someone—anyone—would actually want to talk to a serial killer, but judging from Rocky's interest in the Bloody Murder club, this wasn't a surprise.

"'No calls.'" Cord said, reading God's answer aloud. "'But we can chat here. I'll answer your questions, give you stuff to put in that blog of yours, and in turn you'll help me.'"

"'Help you how?'" This was Rocky's return text.

"'I need to switch to a different phone,'" Cord said, reading the killer's response. "'I'm ditching this one so don't text this number. You'll get another message soon.'"

There were no other messages from God, but Cord went through the cache. There were literally dozens of them, some even to Karina when she'd been in the process of hiring Rocky.

And then she saw the message from an unknown caller. It was buried in the middle of plenty of others, but the first line caused Cord to stop.

"'It's me, again. God. And I have a problem. I'd wanted you to help me with someone playing around with my name, but there's something bigger for you to do right now. The cops think they have the Moonlight Strangler. They don't, and I don't want anyone getting credit for my handiwork. Have one of your club buddies fix that, now, or the next woman I kill will be somebody you know and love.'"

Karina froze. Cord didn't, though. He read through it again. Then, again, before he cursed and leaned in to have a closer look at the small print with the date and time the message had been sent.

"Hell," Cord said, passing the phone to her.

Her heart thumped in her chest. Because the date of the message was two days after Willie Lee's capture. While Willie Lee had been in a coma.

"This is the proof that he's innocent," Karina insisted.

"No," Cord insisted right back. "It could be just another groupie or club member pretending to be the Moonlight Strangler."

She wanted to remind Cord that he'd known about the necklace, but she herself had already dismissed it as proof positive. Still, Karina wanted to believe it.

"The texts will be analyzed," Cord reminded her. He looked at her then. "If the FBI finds something and it turns out that Willie Lee is innocent, then we'll deal with it."

Coming from him that was a huge concession. Huge. "You're having doubts about his guilt?" she asked.

"No. But I want to have doubts." He cursed again, and scrubbed his hand over his face. "And that's why I shouldn't be backing you against a wall and kissing you."

It was true. It was clouding both their minds at a time when cloudy thinking could get them killed.

Especially with the Moonlight Strangler still out there.

Cord's phone rang, the sound slicing through the room and causing her to gasp. She hated the nerves, hated that they almost certainly wouldn't be going away until this was all settled.

Whenever that would be.

"It's Jax," Cord informed her, and he answered the call.

"We got a big problem," Jax said the moment he came on the line. "Two of them, actually. Rocky escaped."

Sweet heaven. That was not what she wanted to hear. Ditto for Cord.

"How the hell did that happen?" Cord snapped.

"The cruiser was attacked on the way into town. Someone shot out the tires, tossed in some tear gas. When Dexter and Mack were coughing their heads off, the attackers rushed in and took Rocky at gunpoint."

Cord shook his head. "Someone *kidnapped* Rocky?"

"Or else someone wanted to make it look that way."

Yes, that was possible, but it didn't matter about the why. Rocky was on the loose again.

However, Karina also thought about what else Jax had told them at the beginning of the call. "You said there were two problems?"

"Yeah." That's all Jax said for several long seconds. "The sheriff over in Comal County just found another body. A woman. She'd been strangled and had a crescent-shaped cut on her cheek. And there was a message from her killer." Jax paused again. "A message left for Karina and you."

Chapter Ten

Cord hated that he had to drag Karina back to the sheriff's office. Hated even more that she was going through this and had that troubled look in her eyes again. But this latest murder had made it necessary.

That, and the fact that whoever had killed the woman apparently had something he wanted to say to Karina and him.

Cord and Karina, I'm still here.

Considering the words had been cut into the dead woman's body, it was obvious the killer wanted to send them a message.

Message received.

The Moonlight Strangler—or more likely someone pretending to be him—had wanted them to know he wasn't in a coma in a prison hospital, that he was free and killing again. If it was a copycat, it was too bad that the woman had paid for that with her life.

By now, Karina knew the drill about not being out in the open any longer than necessary, and she moved fast when Cord parked in front of the sheriff's office. The moment she was inside, her gaze zoomed around the room until she spotted Jericho. He wasn't hard to find because it was only him and one of the reserve deputies in the squad room. All the others were no doubt tied up with the various legs of this investigation.

"Who's the murdered woman?" she asked right away.

Jericho answered right away, too. "Taryn Wellman."

"Oh, God." She didn't stagger, but it was close.

"Yeah, DeWayne's lover," Jericho added. "I haven't had a chance to follow up on the call Taryn made to me. And I obviously won't be able to talk to her about it now. But DeWayne's on his way here, and judging from the way he carried on when I spoke to him, he's not in a good mood. He thinks this is somehow all our fault."

Cord was so not in the mood to deal with De-Wayne. "How the heck is this our fault?"

"Yours," Jericho amended, pointing at Cord. "He's blaming you specifically for this."

Karina shook her head and sank down into the nearest chair. "DeWayne and Taryn are lovers. And I guess he blames us for the Moonlight Strangler still being out there."

Twenty-four hours ago, Cord would have verbally blasted anyone who accused him of that. But now he was rethinking every single second of the attack a month earlier, where he'd been hit with a stun gun, drugged and then cut. All by the man he believed to be his father and the Moonlight Strangler.

However, there was a problem.

Cord hadn't seen Willie Lee's face, something he'd repeatedly told Jericho and the FBI.

"Hell," Cord said, sitting down beside Karina. "Maybe this is all my fault."

He expected her to give you an I-told-you-so look. But she didn't. Karina simply put her arm around him.

"If the Moonlight Strangler really did set all of this up," she said, "then he set up Willie Lee, too. And he would have made sure that you believed Willie Lee was responsible."

Cord had considered all of that before, but for the first time, it really sank in. He blamed the kisses in part for that. However, that had only brought down a few barriers. The facts stayed the same.

"The FBI had one of their so-called memory recovery experts talk to me," Cord explained to her. "It didn't work, but I think I should try it again."

"I can get that started for you," Jericho offered.

But Cord waved him off. "You've got enough to do." Including yet another death and an escaped prisoner. "I'll take care of it when we're done there." Which hopefully would be soon, but there were still plenty of things he needed to discuss with Jericho.

"Anything on Rocky yet?" Cord asked.

Jericho shook his head. "But the so-called kidnapping was captured on the police camera that was in the cruiser. The two thugs were wearing gas masks and gloves, so there's no visual ID, and they didn't leave any prints behind." Jericho turned the computer screen so they could see it. "And then we have this. I'm not sure what to make of it."

That got Cord moving toward the computer. Karina, too, and the first thing Cord saw was Rocky on the screen. It was a clear shot, the image paused in mid-action and what appeared to be mid-cough. There was one gas-masked guy in front of him. Another behind him. The one behind had a gun aimed at Rocky's head. There was a white cloud of tear gas misting all around them and the cruiser.

"Keep watching and listening," Jericho instructed, and he hit the play button.

Since only Rocky's face was visible, it was easy to focus just on him, but Cord tried to take in the whole picture as the two men moved and shoved Rocky away from the cruiser. They were rough with them, but it could be all for show to make it look convincing.

Which it did.

Because the deputies and Rocky were coughing almost violently, it was hard to hear what else was being said, but Cord hit Pause when Rocky looked directly in the camera and said something. Cord replayed it three times.

"He said, 'Help me,'" Karina said and Cord agreed.

Jericho nodded. "And he really looked as if he means it. I'm thinking Rocky might have gotten in over his head in this murder club. Maybe because he didn't manage to kill Karina like they wanted. If he really did go off searching for her attacker last night like he said, then he could have been going after one of his fellow club members."

Definitely, and that wouldn't have set well with the group.

"I haven't made much progress finding out the names of the other members," Cord explained. "What about the FBI? Can they go after the IP addresses and try to find these idiots?"

"Already put in the request," Jericho assured him, and he reached for the desk phone when it rang.

Cord figured with all that was going on, the call could have been about plenty of things, but then Jericho pulled back his shoulders.

"Really?" he said to the caller, and he pressed the button to put it on speaker. "You're the Moonlight Strangler?"

It was probably a crank call. The FBI had been getting hundreds of them, but Cord still found himself moving closer to the phone. Karina, too. Jericho also hit the record button just in case this turned out to be something more than just a poser out for publicity.

For instance, one of their suspects. Or even someone in the Bloody Murder club. At least now, they'd have the guy's voice on tape so it could be analyzed.

"Cord, you listening?" the caller asked. His voice was a raspy whisper. Barely audible, but Cord had no trouble hearing his own name. However, he couldn't hear anything in the background to give him a clue as to where the guy was.

"I'm here. Now, who the hell are you?" Cord snapped.

"Don't you know?" That voice was a taunt, laced with a mock sweetness that stirred something inside Cord.

Cord shook his head. It didn't matter what he felt. He needed to focus on the man doing this.

"Well, I know you're calling yourself the Moonlight Strangler." Cord added some mock sweetness to his tone, too. "But you can't be him because we already have him in custody."

"No, you don't," the man quickly answered. "You have a moron in that prison hospital. Willie Lee Samuels hasn't got the guts to kill. Didn't Karina tell you that?" He didn't wait for an answer. "Of course she did. But you didn't believe her."

"I don't believe you, either," Cord assured him.

"But you will." The caller let that hang in the air for several long moments. "Let's play a little memory game. When you were three years old, you were abandoned at a gas station, and your sister, Addie, was found near the Appaloosa Pass Ranch—"

Cord huffed. "Everybody knows that."

"True. But not everybody knows that Addie was wearing a yellow dress with little flowers on it. And you had on blue overalls and a white shirt. There was a stain on the left sleeve."

Cord felt as if someone had punched him.

Because it was true.

"They didn't put that in the newspapers, did they?" the caller went on, and he gave Cord another dose of that taunting tone. "I know what you were wearing because I was there that day. With you, Addie and your mama. You looked me straight in the eyes, boy, and you saw what I did. Yet you still think Willie Lee is the Moonlight Strangler?"

"Are you okay?" Karina whispered to him, and she took hold of his hand.

No, he wasn't okay. Not by a long shot. The flashback came, staying right at the fringes of his memory. And maybe not a real memory at all. Cord had gone over all the details so many times that maybe he was imagining that day.

But the caller certainly wasn't.

Had Cord really looked into his eyes that day?

"What did I see you do?" Cord heard himself ask.

"Think. It'll all come back to you."

Cord repeated his question, shouting this time, and he hated that this monster had caused him to lose control. The laugh didn't help, either. It was as sickening as the rest of this conversation.

"I'm sending you a gift," the man continued without addressing Cord's question. Or his outburst. "It should be there real soon. After you've had a chance to look at it, we'll talk again."

And with that, he hung up.

Cord sat there, trying to pull himself back together. Hard to do, though. Because if the caller was telling the truth about those clothes—and he was—then, was the other thing the truth, too?

Had Cord really looked him in the eyes?

Maybe, but that wasn't even the worst of it.

"I'm guessing you have no idea what he claims that you saw?" Jericho asked.

"No." And Cord had undergone all kinds of treatments to recover those memories, as well. Including some drug that a behavioral scientist had given him.

A drug meant to pull out those memories of a three-year-old boy, and he'd remembered nothing except a white teddy bear and some Christmas lights.

Hardly a revelation.

But it had been an actual memory because Addie had recalled the same thing. Maybe that meant more memories would come. Even the ones that Cord wasn't sure he wanted to remember.

Had the Moonlight Strangler murdered someone while Cord watched?

As a lawman, he cursed that. And the memories that were so close to the surface, but not clear enough for him to recall them. They could put an end to all his questions. But then, they could also give him plenty of doubts about Willie Lee's guilt.

Hell.

Would this never end?

Jericho gave a heavy sigh and took out his phone. "I'll get someone from the bomb squad down here ASAP. If this clown is really sending you something, I want to make sure it doesn't blow up in our faces."

Cord agreed, and he stood, easing Karina to her feet next to him. "While we're waiting, I'll take Karina to the break room and maybe find her something to eat."

Cord knew he couldn't put anything in his stomach, but maybe he could convince her that she needed to keep up her strength. While he was at it, maybe he could also convince her that he was okay.

He wasn't.

And she knew it.

"There are some sandwiches in the fridge back there," Jericho told them. "Help yourself," he added before he went back to his call.

"Just try taking deep breaths or something," Karina whispered to him. "It won't stop whatever's going on in your head right now, but it'll make you feel as if you're doing something to get past it."

He nodded, and managed to mumble a "thanks."

"But you're going to be all right," she said. "Aren't you?"

Cord stopped, looked at her and was about to give her a reassurance that he darn sure didn't feel. But it seemed stupid to lie to her. They weren't lovers, but they'd been through hell and back together, and if there were any barriers still left between them, it wouldn't be long before they were shot to hell, too.

"What if I was wrong about Willie Lee?" he asked her. A simple question, but he was afraid there were no simple answers.

But somehow Karina managed to find one. "Then, we'll fix it. And then we'll find the real killer." She brushed a kiss on his mouth, slipped her arm around his waist and got them moving toward the break room.

They didn't get far.

The front door opened, and Cord heard a voice he didn't want to hear.

"I told you this would happen," Harley called out to them. "I warned you that somebody would try to kill you again."

Karina turned around to face him. The breath she

took was a weary one. "So you did. Why are you here, Harley?"

"Because I don't want to die." His attention shifted to Cord. "And I want you to do something to find this snake that keeps killing people. Why would you let your number one suspect escape like that?"

"Rocky's just one of our suspects," Cord said to clarify. "But then so are you."

Harley practically snapped to attention. "Me? How do you figure that?"

"Karina's going to testify against you," Cord quickly explained. "You could want her out of the way. Plus, there's that history you say you have with Willie Lee. Any chance you two were involved in money laundering back in the day?"

With all the scars on Harley's face, it was hard to see much change in his expression. But Cord saw it in his eyes. He'd struck a nerve.

"Money laundering?" Harley challenged.

"Don't play innocent," Cord warned him. "It was all over the news recently. No way that you could have missed it."

Of course, it was possible that neither Harley nor Willie Lee truly had anything to do with that operation, but Harley had been looking for something in Willie Lee's cabin. And in Cord's experience, when a man was willing to commit a crime to find something, it was because he was covering up something.

Jericho hit another nerve with Harley, too.

"I just got your background check," Jericho said to Harley. "You were a demolitions expert in the army.

Considering that someone blew up an ambulance last night, I have to wonder if you had anything to do with it."

Yeah, definitely a nerve.

"Anything else you have to say to me, you say through my lawyer. My wife and I keep several on retainer." Harley didn't spare any of them even a glance. He stormed out.

Karina shook her head. "Did he get those scars in the army?"

Jericho shrugged. "I don't know, yet. The army hasn't sent his full military service record, only his career field. In fact, I don't have much more on him at all."

Cord recognized that tone. A suspicious lawman. And it occurred to him that while they knew quite a bit about Rocky and DeWayne, they knew very little about Harley.

"He has a degree in psychology," Jericho said. "He used his GI Bill to go to college at A and M. After that, he dropped off the radar for a while. That's about the same time that big money-laundering scheme was going on."

Too bad the records for that were sketchy at best. "Does he actually have a job now?" Cord asked.

"No. Doesn't need it what with his wife's money. But that money comes with strings attached. There's a prenup, and if she divorces Harley over this B and E scandal, he won't get a penny. Plus, it'd be an even bigger scandal if he's linked to the money-laundering scheme."

Jericho was about to say more, but he reached for his gun. Cord and the deputy went for theirs, too, and Cord pivoted in the direction of the door. But it wasn't the threat his body had prepared him for.

It was a kid.

A girl, no more than eleven or twelve years old.

The guns nearly had her bolting, but Jericho, the deputy and Cord quickly reholstered. Jericho motioned for her to come in. She did, but she took her time with her gaze firing at all of them.

"It's okay," Jericho assured them. "That's Annabeth, and her dad's the cook at the diner."

"Someone left this on one of the tables," she said, holding up an envelope. "It's addressed to the Appaloosa Pass sheriff's office, and my dad told me to bring it right over."

Cord doubted this was a coincidence. It had to be from the caller who'd shaken him to the core. He figured that was just the beginning, though.

"We didn't see who left it there," the girl went on. "We've had a lot of customers in and out all morning, and someone had stuck it between the salt and pepper shakers. Not exactly hidden, you know, but not right out in the open, either."

Because whoever had left it had wanted it to be found. Just not while he was there. Cord made a note to check the security cameras in the area to see if they could spot the person. Again, though, the person had likely covered their tracks.

Jericho put on some latex gloves that he grabbed from a desk drawer, went closer and took it from the girl, but he only touched the edges of the envelope. He was trying to preserve any evidence that might be on it.

Cord figured there wouldn't be any. Not if this guy was the real Moonlight Strangler. Other than that DNA—which was now under suspicion—he'd left no part of himself behind.

Jericho thanked the girl, and she took off, clearly ready to get out of there, and the three of them looked at the envelope. It was indeed addressed to the sheriff's office. No return address. No stamp. And it wasn't sealed.

Cord could see the edges of a photograph, and Jericho took out a note. It had been typed and was only one sentence.

"'Cord, everything you need to know about yourself, and me, is right here.'"

Chapter Eleven

Karina held her breath while Jericho eased the first of the three photos from the envelope. She could practically feel Cord trying to bolster himself for whatever he was about to see. Unfortunately, he might need some bolstering.

"Remember," Karina whispered to him, "anything the person says or gives you could be a lie. We're not dealing with a sane, normal person here."

But she had no idea exactly who they were dealing with, and she doubted anything in that envelope would tell them, either. If the real Moonlight Strangler had indeed sent this, then she figured there would be nothing to incriminate him.

So, why had he sent it?

Jericho carefully placed the photo on the desk, and Karina got a good look at the one on top. It was an old Polaroid, yellow with age and worn in spots, but the image was still fairly clear. It wasn't a posed shot. There was a woman on a porch. Her head was down so it was hard to see much of her face, but she had her hand on her throat and was looking down at two children.

A boy and a girl.

Cord jerked back his shoulders. And Karina knew why. The children were wearing clothes exactly like the ones the caller had described. The clothes that Cord and Addie had been wearing the day they disappeared.

Someone had written "Mom" at the bottom of the photo.

Oh, God.

Was that actually Cord's mother?

Jericho took out another pair of gloves when Cord reached for it, and Cord put them on without taking his attention off the photo.

"That's Addie," Jericho concluded. "I was eight years old the day they found her wandering around the woods near the ranch, and she looked exactly like that. Well, except when they found her, she had a cut on her cheek. She doesn't have one in the photo."

Not yet. Karina had the sickening feeling that it'd come shortly thereafter. And the cut had been the crescent shape that the Moonlight Strangler had given all his victims.

Or in the cases of Addie and herself, his near victims.

Cord picked up the picture and brought it closer, his eyes combing over every inch of it. Especially the woman's face. "I don't remember this. I don't remember *her*."

Since there was nothing she could say to make this

better for him, Karina simply put her arm around him and hoped that helped. It did.

Until Jericho went to the second photo.

Cord actually staggered back a step, and it took him a second to regain his composure. Karina didn't even try to regain hers. Because the photo turned her stomach.

It was the same woman who'd been in the previous shot, but she wasn't on the porch with the kids in this one.

She was dead.

Karina didn't have a lot of experience looking at dead bodies, but the woman was ashen, not a drop of color on her face. Except for that obscene cut on her face and the bruises on her neck.

"It could have been faked," Jericho quickly pointed out. "I'll have the crime lab examine it, but that could be makeup."

Yes, it could be, but Karina doubted it. Judging from the profanity Cord said under his breath, so did he. Like her, he believed he was looking at the face of his dead mother.

"The Moonlight Strangler told Addie that our mother was dead," Cord added.

Karina looked at Jericho to see if he knew about that, and he nodded. "The snake called her months ago to tell her that he wasn't going after her, that she was safe. But he also said her mom was dead."

"Did he kill her?" Karina blurted out before she could stop herself. She wished she had stopped herself because she wasn't sure it was an answer Cord would want to hear.

Jericho shrugged. "He mentioned something about spilling blood."

She was glad she hadn't been around for that call, and even though Cord and Addie had had months now to come to terms with it and everything else they'd learned, they must have had their doubts that the killer was telling them the truth. Or rather their hopes that he was lying.

And maybe he still was.

Karina was going to hang on to that, and she prayed Cord would do the same. They were dealing with a serial killer here, and if he could murder all those women, it wouldn't be much of a stretch for him to lie.

After looking at the first two photos, Karina wasn't sure she wanted to see the third one. Mercy, she hoped it wasn't one of the kids being harmed.

But it wasn't.

The third photo was nothing like the other two. It was a man. And it was someone she instantly recognized.

Willie Lee.

Now, it was Karina's turn to feel as if someone had put a knife in her.

He was young, probably still in his late twenties, but Karina had no doubts that it was Willie Lee. None.

It appeared to be a selfie shot. The lens was close to his face. No smile. His mouth was set in a tight line, and he was holding up something next to his cheek.

A knife.

Oh, God.

A knife!

Karina heard the hoarse groan tear from her throat, and she fumbled around behind her until she found a chair. Cord was right there, helping her sit, and despite the jolt he'd just gotten from his mother's photo, he managed to look a lot steadier than she felt.

"Again, the photo could be fake or doctored," Jericho reminded them both. "Or Willie Lee could have been forced to pose like that."

It was the first time Jericho had even hinted that Willie Lee might be innocent, and if this had been any other time, Karina would have considered it a victory. Not now, though.

Not after seeing that knife.

"I think I should go ahead and take Karina back to the ranch," Cord said.

She didn't argue. Couldn't. It felt as if someone had taken hold of her heart and was crushing it. Besides, the person who'd sent those photos could still be nearby. Just the thought of that was too much for her to handle.

Cord helped her to her feet, but before they could make it to the door, she saw someone else she didn't want to see.

DeWayne.

No. Cord and she had been through enough today without adding this.

Of course, Jericho had said DeWayne was on his way to the sheriff's office, but what with the phone call and those photos, she'd forgotten all about it.

And she didn't have the energy to deal with DeWayne right now.

"On second thought, I'll take Karina to the break room," Cord said. Probably because his truck was parked right out front. Exactly where DeWayne was walking. That would mean running right into the man.

Jericho gathered up the photos, note and envelope and put them in a clear plastic bag that he then placed in the desk drawer. No doubt so that DeWayne wouldn't see them. But then it occurred to her that DeWayne might have known all about them because he could have been the one who sent them.

Heck, she was latching on to Jericho's theory that the photos could have been faked. DeWayne could have done that.

That gave her some much-needed strength, and she didn't go running to the break room when DeWayne walked in. Even though judging from the scowl Cord gave her, that's exactly what he had wanted her to do.

"Taryn's dead," DeWayne snapped, and he looked directly at Karina as if she was the one responsible.

"Yes, I heard. And I'm sorry." She meant that. Karina was indeed sorry about the woman's murder, but that's where her sympathy ended. "Were you the one who killed her?"

"Kill her?" DeWayne asked, his voice practically a shout. "She was my lover. Why would I want her dead?"

Karina could think of several reasons, but Cord spoke before she could voice them.

"Because you want to make yourself look innocent of being the real Moonlight Strangler," Cord said. "Or maybe because Taryn learned something about you and you wanted to silence her."

The anger shot through DeWayne's eyes. And not just ordinary anger. Rage. "You have no proof of any of that, and you're grasping at straws." He jabbed his index finger at Karina. "And it's because of her. Because you're sleeping with her, and she's been feeding you lies."

"No, it's because I'm a lawman, and I can see there's a problem here. You're covering up something. It could be your involvement in that old money-laundering operation—"

"I don't have to listen to this," DeWayne interrupted, throwing his hands in the air. "I came here to find out what she knows about Taryn's murder." Karina got another finger jab in her direction.

Karina didn't even pause. "I don't know anything about it. Well, nothing except that it appears she was either murdered by the Moonlight Strangler or by someone who wants us to believe she was. Since you believe Willie Lee is the serial killer, then maybe you just lost your temper with Taryn, killed her and then decided to go with the copycat buzz that's all over town."

"I know something," Jericho volunteered. "Taryn called me earlier to say you'd been acting suspicious and that she thought you were being blackmailed or *something*. Want to talk about that?"

The question clearly threw DeWayne. No rage this

time. He seemed to be sizing up Jericho to see if he was telling the truth. He must have decided he was because his shoulders dropped.

"Taryn was wrong," DeWayne finally said, "and she shouldn't have talked to you." But then, his head snapped up, his attention going back to Karina. "Did you say anything about Taryn to those Bloody Murder club guys? Because one of them could have killed her."

"I haven't spoken to any of them," Karina answered. But then she rethought that. Maybe she had. Maybe she was talking to one of them now. Or Harley could be a member, too.

DeWayne made a sound of outrage. "I don't know how you did it, but you're responsible for this."

"Enough," Cord declared. He took hold of her arm and led her toward Jericho's office.

She expected DeWayne to follow them. And he tried. But Jericho stepped in front of him. "Let's have a discussion about Taryn's call. I want your statement on the record."

Karina didn't wait to see how DeWayne would react to that. Cord didn't let her. He took her into Jericho's office and shut the door.

"I'm sorry," she said at the same moment Cord said it, too.

Despite the hellish things they'd just seen in those photos, he smiled. Not for long, though. "I need to talk to Addie," Cord said. "And tell her about the pictures."

He was obviously dreading it. With good reason.

It wouldn't be an easy conversation, especially when he told her about the dead woman in the photo.

"Addie will probably want to see the pictures for herself," Karina suggested. She would want to see them if she was in Addie's shoes. Karina only hoped Addie could "unsee" them after that.

Cord nodded. "Maybe the photos will trigger something in her memory."

Though he didn't sound pleased about that. Still, Addie might be able to tell them something about the photos that they didn't know. Since Addie and Cord were twins and had therefore been the same age, maybe Addie could remember some fragments of that day.

Cord pulled her to him, bringing her right into his arms. Not for a kiss this time. He just held her.

Like the other times she'd been close to him like this, the heat came. Slowly consumed her. But there was more to it now. The heat didn't cloud her mind. It gave her some clarity.

She was falling hard for him.

Not exactly something that she should be doing, but Karina didn't know how to stop it. Oh, mercy. It wouldn't be long before she would have to deal with a broken heart in addition to all these other memories from the attacks and the deaths.

Cord pulled back, their gazes connecting. For a moment, she thought that kiss might happen after all. But it didn't.

"Why did he send us those pictures?" he asked.

Because of the sheer shock of seeing the photos,

Karina hadn't questioned it. She should have, though. "To shake us up, to keep us off balance?"

Cord gave another nod. "And that must mean we're getting close. Too close." He glanced between them, and she didn't think he was just talking about a serial killer now.

Was he talking about them?

Karina didn't get a chance to find out because there was a knock at the door, and a split second later, Jericho opened it. Cord and she stepped apart, as if they'd been caught doing something wrong.

However, Jericho didn't even seem to have noticed, and if he did, he didn't mention the close contact between Cord and her.

"DeWayne's gone," Jericho explained. "I threatened again to put him in a holding cell, and that got him moving." He held up a notepad. "I just got a call from a military record's rep, and he gave me some more info about Harley."

That got her mind off the broken-heart possibility. It got Cord's attention, too.

"Harley's scars are from an accident. A live explosive that he mishandled. This happened forty years ago when he was just nineteen. After his injuries healed, he failed a psych exam and was discharged from the army."

A failed psych exam wasn't good, but then maybe it didn't mean anything. After all, Harley was just a teenager then, and anyone who'd gone through that would have been altered for life.

"Is there a record of Willie Lee ever being in the army with him?" Karina asked.

"Well, Willie Lee was in the army, only for six months, though, before he was given a medical discharge for bad knees. Harley and he were in training at the same time in South Carolina."

So, maybe that's how they'd met. Karina carried that one step further. Harley and he could have reconnected after Harley's discharge. Maybe even gotten involved with money laundering. But there was still no proof of that.

Or was there?

The memory came to her in a flash. "Years ago, I remember seeing Willie Lee burning something. He had an old oil barrel outside his cabin, and he would sometimes burn paid bills and such. He said it was better than buying a shredder. But that time, it looked as if he was burning a book."

"A book?" Cord questioned.

"Not a regular book. Smaller. Like maybe a journal or something."

Cord stayed quiet a moment. "Did you ask him about it?"

"No." And Karina remembered why. "Willie Lee always got this look on his face when he didn't want to talk about something. And he had that look then, so I didn't say anything about it."

But she certainly thought about it now. Had it really been a journal? With perhaps something in it about the money laundering?

Jericho's phone rang, and he was cursing the interruption before he took out his phone. However, the cursing stopped when he looked at the screen.

"It's the prison," Jericho said.

He didn't put the call on speaker, and Karina wasn't close enough to him to hear what the caller was saying. However, she could tell something had happened.

Probably something bad.

That's the way their luck had been running since this whole ordeal had started.

Karina tried to rein in her fears, but she failed. Thankfully, the conversation didn't last long, only a few seconds, but even after he pressed the button to end the call, Jericho continued to stare at his phone.

"That was the prison hospital," Jericho finally said. "Willie Lee just came out of his coma."

Chapter Twelve

Cord still wasn't sure that coming to the prison hospital was the right thing to do. Not with Karina anyway. But he hadn't been able to talk her, or himself, out of letting Jericho handle this.

He had to face his birth father. And get some answers to all those questions that'd been haunting him for years.

Well, he'd get answers anyway. But Cord wasn't sure he could believe anything Willie Lee told him.

Of course, Willie Lee wasn't the only elephant in the room. There was the question of Karina's safety. That's why Jericho had told Mack to follow them in a cruiser. It was broad daylight so maybe they wouldn't be ambushed, but the earlier attack had happened in broad daylight, too. Better to be safe than sorry, so Mack was waiting outside in the prison parking lot and would follow them back to Appaloosa Pass when they were done.

Without saying a word to each other, Karina and he made their way through security and the maze of corridors, each closed off with its own bars. An in-the-face reminder that this was maximum security. And that Willie Lee was here for a darn good reason.

They made it all the way to the hospital section before Karina stepped in front of him, stopping Cord in his tracks. Cord had been waiting for this, waiting for her to say that no matter what happened, they'd get through this. Or else she'd put a different spin on that pep talk.

But she didn't.

She just leaned in and kissed him. "I think we should sleep together."

All right. Well, he sure as heck hadn't seen that coming. "Now? Here?"

Karina smiled, making him smile, too. Though there really wasn't anything to smile about. Except for her. For some reason, she just kept making him smile.

Kept distracting him, too.

"Well, I was thinking later would be better timing," she answered. "You know, after we've survived this."

Survived. That was a good word for it. She'd survived three physical attacks, a whole host of verbal ones, too. Now, this chat with Willie Lee. If the man confessed to being the Moonlight Strangler, it would tear her world apart.

"We're still not on the same side here," Cord reminded her.

She kissed him again. "We don't have to be. We just have to get through this." She slipped her hand in his.

And Cord knew she was right. One step at a time.

Get through this. Put an end to the danger. Then, he'd definitely haul her off to bed. Even if it meant complicating the hell out of things.

Which it would.

Maybe this fire he felt for her would cool some after their chat with Willie Lee. Or not, Cord amended when he glanced at her.

He finally got them moving again, and when they reached the next security checkpoint, a woman wearing green scrubs was there to greet them. According to her name tag, she was Dr. Dana Kenney.

"I wasn't sure you would come," the doctor said to Cord. "I understand you're his son?"

"Biological son," Cord automatically amended. He tipped his head to Karina. "And Willie Lee has worked for Karina for years."

"He's a friend," Karina said. An automatic correction for her as well that had the doctor staring at them and then clearing her throat.

"Well, I have good news and bad," the doctor continued. "Yes, Willie Lee is awake, and he's nearly healed from the gunshot wounds to his chest."

Wounds that Cord had given him. The doctor didn't mention that, but she likely knew. If they wanted to swap stories, Cord could have shown her his own scars from that day.

"And the bad news?" Karina prompted when the doctor paused.

"His blood pressure is way too high, and his memory is all muddled. The medical term for it is dissociative amnesia, probably brought on by the trauma of being shot."

Cord cursed. "Or he could be faking it."

The doctor didn't hesitate before she nodded. "And it's also possible the medications he's been receiving are contributing to the problem. We're weaning him off the meds now so we might see an improvement in a day or two."

Cord could see the frustration in Karina's eyes. "Please tell me we don't have to wait that long to see him," Karina said.

"No. You can see him. This way." The doctor began to lead them down yet another corridor. "Just don't expect too much. And you can always come back later this week."

Cord didn't want to wait another second, much less days. Willie Lee had to give them something to stop these attacks. They might not get so lucky if there was another one.

"Has Willie Lee said anything to you?" Karina asked the doctor.

"Nothing about his arrest if that's what you want to know. But then he just started talking right before you got here. He's had a tube down his throat so he might be still experiencing some pain when he moves any of the muscles required for speech."

Cord felt the anger swell inside him. Each thing the doctor said sounded like some kind of excuse. Of course, his anger was mixed with a whole laundry list of other things that Cord wished he didn't feel.

The doctor took them into a large room. Not a

usual hospital room, either. This one had multiple beds, all empty, and along with some cameras, there was also a guard. Standing right over the sole prisoner in the room.

Willie Lee.

"I'll wait here," the doctor said, motioning for them to go closer. "Don't touch him and keep at least two feet away from the bed."

Rules. But Willie Lee didn't look in any shape to attack anyone. Of course, maybe the doctor was worried about Cord doing the attacking.

Willie Lee was in the bed, machines all around him, covered from neck to toes in bleached white sheets. The man didn't have much more color in his face, either.

Cord had never actually gotten a good look at him. When he'd shot Willie Lee a month ago, it had been from a distance while Cord had been drugged and bleeding. After the shooting, Cord had been whisked away in one ambulance, Willie Lee in another.

But Cord sure saw him now when he went closer to the bed.

His first thought was the man looked a lot older than fifty-nine. His hair was threaded with gray, and his face was hollow. Cord couldn't see a bit of himself in the man.

Until Willie Lee opened his eyes.

Ah, hell. There it was—that punch of recognition. Because both Addie's and his eyes were a genetic copy of Willie Lee's.

Willie Lee blinked several times as if trying to

focus, and his attention landed on Karina. He smiled. Tried to speak. But it was definitely recognition that Cord saw in those troublesome eyes. If Willie Lee did indeed have amnesia, then it was pretty darn selective.

"Karina," the man finally said. He winced, maybe in pain. Maybe pretending.

Cord wasn't giving him the benefit of the doubt just yet, though there were times when Cord's wounds still gave him more than a twinge or two.

Willie Lee's wincing turned to a frown, and he reached out toward her as if to touch her cheek. He didn't make it far because his hands were in restraints. Puzzled, he looked at those, too.

"What happened to you?" Willie Lee asked. "Who hurt you?"

"I'm fine. It's just a scratch. How are you?"

That last part was the usual question someone would ask when visiting a friend in the hospital, but she was blinking, too. Not to get her focus but to fight back the tears.

Willie Lee shook his head. "Why am I here?"

"You were shot. Do you remember?"

"No," he answered after a long pause. "Are the horses okay? Did something happen to them? You look really sad."

Karina moistened her lips before she said anything. "I'm sad because you were hurt. And because you're here. You're in a prison hospital," she added a heartbeat later.

His forehead bunched up. Willie Lee glanced around

the room as if seeing it for the first time, and then his gaze finally settled on Cord. "Who are you?"

Easy question. Tough answer. Especially now that Cord had a blasted lump in his throat. Best not to sugarcoat this. Cord just put it out there. "According to a DNA test, you're my biological father."

Willie Lee shook his head again, his stare never leaving Cord. Then, the head shaking stopped. Like Karina, his eyes filled with tears. "You're actually my son?"

Best to add this, as well. "Yeah, and you have a daughter. Her name is Addie, and someone—probably you—abandoned us when we were only three years old. But I guess you're going to say you don't remember her, either?"

Willie Lee didn't jump to respond, but he did close his eyes, and he groaned. Even Cord had to admit it was a pitiful sound. However, he didn't let it get to him. He needed to ask some questions.

Well, one big question anyway, but Willie Lee spoke before Cord could even continue.

"Your mother," Willie Lee said. Not a question. And the tears weren't just in his eyes now. They were streaming down his cheeks. "She's dead?"

Now, that last part was definitely a question.

"I believe she could be," Cord answered. If those photos weren't fake, that is. "Did you kill her?"

"No." Willie Lee's chest dropped with a heavy sigh, and he repeated, "No."

He made another sound. Pain mixed with grief. Maybe the real deal since it seemed like something too intense to be faked. Of course, the grief could be there because Willie Lee regretted murdering her.

"I loved her," Willie Lee said a moment later. "She was a good woman. Her name was Sarah."

Cord latched on to the name as if it was a lifeline. He knew so little about her, and other than her name and those two pictures, he still didn't know much. Later, there'd be time to question the man about that.

"Are you the Moonlight Strangler?" Cord asked.

Willie Lee's eyes widened. "I don't think so. Am I?"

"I'm the one asking you," Cord returned.

But if the comment even got through to him, Willie Lee showed no signs of it. "Your mother was murdered, wasn't she?" he went on. A sob tore from his mouth, and he broke down, crying.

Since the man's memory seemed to be pretty good on the subject of his dead wife, Cord figured it was time to repeat the real question.

Are you the Moonlight Strangler?

The words seemed to freeze in his mind, though, when Willie Lee opened his eyes and looked at him. "You're the one who shot me," he said. "I remember that now. But why?"

Cord decided to show him. He unbuttoned his shirt but didn't need to look down to know what Willie Lee—and Karina—was seeing. The two scars. Nowhere near healed, but they weren't the raw mess they had been. Still, he'd carry them for life.

"Mercy," Karina whispered, and she'd gone almost as pale as Willie Lee.

Cord hadn't intended to shock her like that. Heck, he hadn't intended for her to see them, period, and he gave her a whispered apology.

However, he had no apology for Willie Lee.

"You did that to me," Cord snapped, yanking the sides of his shirt back together with far more force than necessary. "And now you say you don't remember cutting me and tying my leg with a rope?"

"I don't think he's lying about that," the doctor interrupted. She walked toward them. "According to the tox screen sent from the Appaloosa Pass Hospital, Willie Lee had been pumped full of barbiturates when he was admitted."

Cord dropped back a mental step. He hadn't known that about Willie Lee. Hadn't bothered to ask once he found out that the man hadn't regained consciousness before he was taken into custody.

"That could affect his memory?" Karina asked.

The doctor nodded. "Especially with the large amount he had in his system."

Yeah, it could. And Cord knew that firsthand because his captor had dosed him with barbiturates, too. A boatload of them. It'd been a miracle that Cord had managed to take aim at, much less shoot Willie Lee.

Karina looked at Cord. "You said you had broken memories of that day, too."

"Yes," he admitted. "There aren't many details between being hit with a stun gun and then turning up by the old church where I shot Willie Lee."

"And you don't think it's strange that both of you were drugged?" Karina queried.

"Of course I do, but Willie Lee could have drugged himself when he realized he was about to be captured."

Or maybe someone else had done that to him. There was only one way to find out.

Cord didn't hesitate with the question this time. "Are you the Moonlight Strangler?"

It was as if the world exploded. The machines started beeping like crazy, and Willie Lee threw back his head, his body going stiff and his face stretching like some kind of sick death mask.

"He's having a seizure," the doctor said, urgency in her voice and movements. She shoved Cord and Karina to the side so she could get to her patient. "You two need to wait in the hall. Go, now!"

But Cord's feet seemed glued to the floor. Was Willie Lee faking this? If so, it looked darn real.

"Come on." Karina took his hand and got them moving out of there.

They went back into the hall, and Cord hoped he didn't do something wussy, like lose his lunch. He could feel every nerve inside him, and even though he'd never remembered having his mother in his life, her loss had hit him hard. Much as it had done to Willie Lee.

Cord hadn't forgotten that all of this had to be affecting Karina, but he didn't realize just how much until their gazes met. Hell. She was crying and no doubt on the verge of losing more than her lunch. She loved Willie Lee, and it must have cut her to the core to see, and hear, all of that.

"I'm sorry," Cord said, pulling her into his arms.

She didn't break down exactly, but she made some hiccupping sounds when she tried to gather her breath. "If he's the one who cut you like that…"

Karina didn't finish. No need. But it did let him know just how much his scars had affected her. He'd curse himself for that later, but for now he just held her and tried to undo the damage.

"I'm fine," he assured her. And that was only a partial lie. "I'll be returning to duty in a week." Once he cleared the Justice Department shrink who'd be assigned to evaluate him. "They wouldn't let me go back to work if I wasn't a hundred percent."

She pulled back, looked at him again. There was a new set of trouble in her eyes. "I didn't realize you'd be leaving so soon."

Ah, that. And here just minutes earlier they'd discussed having sex. Judging from that look in her eyes, she was thinking he'd meant for their theoretical lovemaking to be a one-night stand.

And hell, it might be.

But Cord wasn't even ready to go there yet.

"I won't be leaving the area," he explained. "Well, I will be given a desk job somewhere, but I won't be going back in the field."

Karina stared at him, probably waiting for more. Or maybe she just wanted something else to fill her mind so she wouldn't have to think about what was going on in the room behind them.

Willie Lee could be dying. Or already dead.

"I was a Joe," Cord went on. "A deep cover operative. Once I stayed undercover on the same assignment for two years." A drug-dealing operation that he wouldn't discuss with her. Not with anyone. He'd been lucky not to get PTSD, but those were memories he didn't want to poke, either.

"I just thought, well, I thought you'd want to be closer to Addie."

"I do." And he did. Close to his nephew, too. Heck, after this ordeal, he was starting to feel as if Jericho and he had forged some kind of peace treaty.

The door behind them opened, and after Cord got one glimpse of the doctor's face, he figured it was time for him to put his arm around Karina again.

"This could take a while," Dr. Kenney said, making some notes in a chart. "He had a grand mal seizure, and his blood pressure hasn't stabilized. There's a café just up the road next to a big gas station," she added. "If you don't want to drive home, you can wait there for a while, and I'll call you if there's any news. The guards have your cell phone number, I'm sure."

Karina caught on to the doctor's arm before she could leave. "How bad is it?" she asked.

"Bad," Dr. Kenney admitted. "I hope you got everything you needed from him because Willie Lee might not make it."

Chapter Thirteen

The chicken club sandwich tasted like dust, but Karina forced herself to eat it anyway. She couldn't make herself sick with worry over Willie Lee. Even though that's exactly what she was doing.

Cord wasn't faring so well, either.

He was on the phone again, something he'd been doing practically since they'd left the jail and had driven to the diner the doctor had recommended. He had hardly more than a bite of his cheeseburger and fries before sliding his plate to Mack. The deputy had his own meal but had mumbled something about getting a to-go box.

Karina thought maybe Cord's latest call was to Jericho, though she couldn't tell much of what was going on since Cord was doing a lot more listening than talking. Of course, he had already told Jericho about the prison visit. Had then called Addie and told her what was going on. That had required him to talk his sister out of making a trip there.

Karina was glad he'd managed to do that.

Even though Addie wanted to see Willie Lee, that

wasn't going to happen until the doctor called them. It was best if Addie was at the ranch, safe with her son and husband. Karina had known from the start that just being out on the road had been a risk, and she didn't want Addie taking that risk, too.

Cord was already dealing with enough without adding his sister's safety to his worries.

"So, Willie Lee never made an actual confession?" Mack asked.

Mack didn't just blurt it out, though. He sounded as if he'd chosen his words carefully and probably had. Had no doubt even debated asking it since they'd been at the diner for nearly a half hour, and he'd only listened to the summary she'd given him of their visit with Willie Lee.

"No confession about the Moonlight Strangler," she confirmed. "But he did admit to being Cord and Addie's father."

Karina had purposely kept her voice to a whisper because the three of them were all together in a booth, but Cord likely heard her because he looked up from his phone conversation and caught her gaze.

"*Biological* father," Karina amended as Cord had done at the hospital.

In her fantasy world, she'd hoped that Willie Lee could resolve everything for all of them. She'd hoped that he could somehow clear his name. Give them the identity of the real killer. And that the real killer could already be behind bars.

But it'd been just that—a fantasy.

Now, Willie Lee could be dead, and any information could die with him. Along with her losing a friend. A man she loved and thought of as family.

"Hey, it's okay." Mack patted her hand. "We're going to work all of this out somehow."

It took a moment for Karina to realize why Mack had done that. It was because she was crying. Again. She wiped away the tears, cursing them, and told herself that they wouldn't return. Tears wouldn't help Willie Lee.

Prayers might, though, and that's why she'd said a few for him.

The fresh round of tears seemed to do the trick for getting Cord off the phone, and he handed her a paper napkin from the metal dispenser.

"No sign of Rocky yet," Cord said right away, and while he kept his attention on her, he gulped down some more coffee. "Two of the reserve deputies are still looking, though."

So, he had been talking to Jericho. "Anything on Taryn's murder?"

He shook his head. "But there's a connection between Rocky and DeWayne. Rocky's father, Frank, and DeWayne were once in business together, and Frank apparently doesn't have good things to say about DeWayne. He said DeWayne got drunk one night and rattled on about an old business deal gone bad with Willie Lee." Cord lifted his shoulder. "It could mean nothing."

And it could be connected to that money-laundering scheme. In fact, Karina wondered if they'd all been involved in some way—DeWayne, Harley. Heck, even

Willie Lee. Maybe that's what'd prompted Harley to break into Willie Lee's cabin.

Cord drank some more coffee and downed a couple of ibuprofen that he'd bought at the counter.

Karina wanted to ask if it was his chest or head hurting. Maybe both. But she doubted he'd tell her the truth. Doubted even more that he'd want to discuss those scars on his chest.

However, they didn't need to discuss it for her to know it was something she'd never forget. God. He'd been through so much. Being abandoned, the attacks, learning that his mother was almost certainly dead. And it wasn't even over.

It might never be over.

"Don't look at me like that," Cord said.

Karina knew what he meant. She was feeling sorry for him, and it showed. She quickly tried to change her expression, but it was too late.

Mack picked up on it, too. "I got to take a trip to the men's room. I won't be long."

But Mack probably would stay away from the booth to give Cord and her a chance to talk. However, Cord didn't say anything. He clammed up after the deputy scurried away.

"I'm okay, really," Cord insisted.

As Mack had done to her, she slid her hand over his. "Liar." She'd hoped that would make him smile, but it didn't work.

"I should have gotten right in Willie Lee's face until he gave me a straight answer about being the Moonlight Strangler." Cord cursed himself. "I'm a federal agent, and I know how to interrogate someone."

"Willie Lee wasn't just *someone*," Karina reminded him. "And besides, even if you had repeated the question, he might not have been able to answer. Something was clearly wrong with him."

Cord stayed quiet a moment, nodded. "Has he ever had a seizure before?"

"Not that I know of. But that doesn't mean it never happened. Like I said, Willie Lee could be secretive." She paused. "He did seem to love your mother, though."

The muscles in his jaw went to war with each other. "Yeah. Maybe if he comes out of this, he can tell us where her body is. I'd like to give her a proper burial. And no, she wasn't any of the other known victims. All of their DNA is in the system now, and it would have hit as a match to Addie and me."

True. But there was also someone else in the DNA pool. Karina had never met him, but it was a man named Lonny Ogden, who was now confined to a psychiatric facility. Months ago, the cops had learned about Ogden, and since he was a match to Cord and Addie, it also meant he was a match to Willie Lee. That meant Willie Lee had three children.

Karina was about to bring that up to Cord, but she could see that he was shutting down again. Already looking at his phone for somebody to call so he wouldn't have to discuss this with her. But his phone rang before he could punch in a number.

"Jericho," he said, and he answered it immediately, probably because the sheriff had gotten some big news to call back so soon.

Cord didn't put it on speaker. There were people eating nearby, but Karina moved closer to him so she could hear.

"The photo is a selfie," Jericho said without even saying a greeting. "Or whatever they called them back when it was taken."

It took Karina a moment to realize what he was talking about. The picture that'd been left in the diner and brought to the sheriff's office.

The picture of Willie Lee.

"He took it himself," Jericho went on. "I faxed the photos to the FBI lab, and they did a rush job. They enhanced the image, and Willie Lee is definitely holding the camera. And the knife. Of course, that doesn't mean someone wasn't there in the room forcing him to do it."

No, but it didn't make him look innocent, either.

"What about the other photos?" Cord asked.

She didn't like Jericho's hesitation that followed. "They did age progression for the one on the porch. It's you and Addie all right, but there was a problem with the woman. They used some kind of facial composite program, and the woman's features didn't match yours and Addie's."

Karina hadn't expected that. Judging from Cord's deep breath, neither had he. "So, she's not our mother?" Cord asked.

"Doesn't appear to be. But of course, that leaves

us with the question of who is she. You think Willie Lee could or would tell us?"

"Maybe," Cord said as if going over that in his mind. He didn't look relieved exactly, but he had to be. Because there was the possibility his mother was still alive. After all, Willie Lee didn't seem as if he knew for sure.

"And as for the final one," Jericho went on, "well, they're pretty sure the woman in the photo—whoever she is—is dead, that it wasn't faked. Are you okay?" he added a moment later.

"I'm fine," Cord answered, after a short hesitation. "How would they know it wasn't faked?"

"It hadn't been doctored. They could tell that, too, because it was a Polaroid, and they're hard to alter without leaving lots of signs. And the woman had classic petechia in her eyes, a sign of strangulation. Plus, she'd been strangled with some kind of wire that had apparently cut through her skin. A deep enough cut that her hyoid bone was likely broken."

So, there it was, all spelled out for them. A woman who'd been in an earlier photo with them had been murdered.

"Still okay?" Jericho asked Cord.

"Does Addie know?" Cord obviously didn't want to answer Jericho's question.

"Not yet. Maybe you two can talk about it soon. I wasn't sure if this would get up her hopes or not about your birth mother, and I thought you might want to wait to tell her until you knew for sure."

Of course, they might never know for sure.

Cord's phone beeped to indicate he had another call coming in. "The prison," Cord said, glancing at the screen. "Jericho, I'll have to call you back."

Cord ended the call with Jericho and took the one from the prison. This time, he did put the call on speaker.

"This is Dr. Kenney," the woman said when Cord greeted her. "Willie Lee's stabilized for now."

Karina's breath rushed out. From the relief. However, Cord wasn't sharing that relief with her. "Good. I need to finish the interrogation—"

"Sorry," the doctor interrupted, "but I'm not allowing him any other visitors today."

"I need to talk to him," Cord snapped.

"I know. And I know he's been accused of some horrible crimes, but he's also my patient. I'm sorry, Agent Granger, but you'll have to wait. I'll give you a call in the morning." The woman hung up so that Cord didn't even get a chance to pressure her.

Cord immediately stood up, finishing off the rest of the coffee and dropping some money on the table. "I'll get Mack," he said.

But the words seemed to die on his lips, and Cord reached for his gun.

Karina whirled around to see what had caused him to do that. And her heart went to her knees.

No.

This couldn't be happening again.

Mack was there all right, but standing behind him was a man wearing a ski mask. He had Mack in a choke hold and held a gun to the deputy's head.

"Everybody out!" the man shouted. "Everybody but you two," he added to Cord and her.

Karina didn't recognize his voice, but there was something familiar about his size and stance. This was almost certainly one of the men who'd taken Rocky at gunpoint.

The diners immediately started to scatter, all running for the door. Cord moved, too, putting himself in front of her and taking aim at the man. However, he didn't have a clean shot.

"I'm sorry," Mack said. "I didn't see him in the bathroom until it was too late. I think he came in through a window."

Which meant he'd probably been watching them, waiting for the right time for this. Whatever *this* was. Did he want her dead?

Karina figured she'd soon find out.

The thug waited, his back against the wall so that no one could sneak up on him. And he watched as the last of the diners hurried out. At least one of them would call the cops if they hadn't already. The thug must have known that so that meant he might start shooting.

"Stay down and behind me," Cord told her without taking his attention off the man.

But Cord wouldn't do that. Again, he would be the one in the direct line of fire. Maybe, just maybe, this snake hadn't been sent there to kill him.

"This all has to happen fast," the man finally said. "I leave with the woman, and both of you get to live."

"No deal," Cord answered without hesitating. "Who sent you to do this?"

The guy actually chuckled. "That kind of information is well above my pay grade. I just do what I'm told, and I expect you to do the same. Let's go. Follow me."

And he started dragging Mack toward the kitchen.

The diner wasn't that large, and the staff had obviously fled. Good. Because Karina didn't want anyone hit by friendly fire.

Especially since she was the target.

God, who wanted her? Maybe she'd find out before this jerk managed to hurt or kill her.

"Move faster," the guy barked.

Cord and she did, and she stayed behind him, looking over her shoulder to make sure no one came in through the front. However, once they got into the kitchen, she saw something else she didn't want to see.

Another hired gun in a ski mask.

He was by the back door and already had it open. She could see a car parked just outside, and that door was also open. They were ready for her.

Her heart was already pounding, but it raced even more. And her breath became so thin that it felt as if she was about to hyperventilate. But she couldn't. If she did, Mack or Cord could die.

She didn't have a weapon, but Karina glanced around for anything she could use. The only thing nearby was a paring knife, but she snatched it up, holding it by her side so that hopefully the thugs wouldn't see it.

"Now, for the tricky part," the first man said. "Karina, come here, and I'll let the deputy go. Scout's honor."

She doubted she could believe anything he said, and Cord must have agreed because he kept in front of her.

"I'll go with you instead," Cord offered.

The guy shook his head. "Sorry, but I've heard about you. You're a big-shot DEA agent. You could probably kick my butt into the next county with some fancy martial arts. No, thanks. If the woman doesn't come over here now, the deputy gets a bullet."

Karina only hesitated a second, but it was obviously too long because the shot blasted through the kitchen.

And Mack yelled out in pain.

The thug had shot him in the arm.

"The next one goes in his belly," the man growled. "Then, his heart. After that, your precious DEA agent takes a bullet to the head and all because you're too stubborn to follow orders."

"I'll go with you," she said, earning her a sharp glare from Cord.

She wasn't sure if he saw the knife she was holding. Or maybe he had and knew it wouldn't be much of a weapon against two armed men. If they got her in that car, they would take her somewhere and kill her.

Maybe even take her to the Moonlight Strangler.

"Don't do this, Karina," Cord insisted. He was volleying glances from Mack, who was grimacing in pain, to the men and then to her.

She connected gazes with the man who was holding Mack, and she could tell from his eyes that he was about to pull the trigger again. This wasn't a bluff, and it didn't help when she heard the police sirens approaching. The thugs were running out of time.

And so was she.

Karina started walking. Not slowly, either. She didn't want to give them a chance to see the knife. The moment she was near the thug, he shoved Mack forward, the deputy falling onto the floor, and he grabbed Karina.

That's when she made her own move.

She brought up the knife, aiming for his neck. But he saw her and tried to knock her hand away. Karina came right back at him, and this time she jammed the knife in his throat. He yelled out, cursing her, and with the blood gushing from his neck, he fell to his knees.

The other man brought up his gun, but it was too late. Cord fired. Two shots. Both of them slamming into the man's chest. He dropped to the floor next to his partner while Mack scrambled away from them.

Karina moved, too, thanks to Cord. Her legs seemed to have stopped working, but he maneuvered her to the other side of the room behind a stainless prep table. That's when Karina looked at her hand. She still held the knife.

And now she had his blood on her.

As horrifying of a sight as that was, she wasn't the only one with blood. Mack had the gunshot wound to his arm, and Karina dropped the knife so she could grab a dish towel and apply some pressure to it. The wound didn't look that bad, but he would need a doctor soon.

There were some sounds in the diner. Then, hurried footsteps. Several seconds later, two uniformed officers came running to the door to peer into the kitchen. Both had their weapons drawn.

"I'm Cord Granger, DEA," he said, taking his badge from his pocket to show them. "We need an ambulance."

"Already on the way," one of the officers assured him. One of the uniforms went toward the thugs. The other stayed near Cord, Mack and her.

"Who are these guys?" the officer asked.

"Hired killers," Cord answered. Good thing because Karina wasn't sure she could speak yet. Cord went to the men, yanking off their ski masks. "Strangers," he added.

That didn't make it any easier to stomach. They'd come close to dying. And now Mack was hurt. All because of her. And Karina still didn't know why.

"Is it clear back there?" someone called out. Another officer probably, because one of the uniforms responded right away.

"It's clear. And there's a DEA agent on scene. Two injuries, though."

Karina shook her head when she realized he was adding her to the injured list. Probably because of her bloody hands and the cuts and bruises she already had.

"I'm not hurt," she said.

"How many dead bodies you got?" the cop in the

diner called out. He came into the doorway of the kitchen. Not a uniform this time. He was in khakis and a white shirt. Probably a detective.

"Two," the officer next to her answered.

The cop in the doorway mumbled something she didn't catch, and he looked around the room until his gaze connected with Cord. "You're the DEA agent?" he asked.

Cord nodded.

The cop hitched his thumb toward the diner. "A woman's out front, and she says she needs to speak to you immediately, that it's important." The cop paused. "She says she's your mother."

Chapter Fourteen

Cord stood there a moment, trying to process what the cop had just told him. He couldn't.

"My mother?" he questioned.

After his conversation with Jericho about the photos, Cord was just coming to terms with the notion that his mother might not be dead. But he sure as heck hadn't expected her to show up at a crime scene.

And maybe she hadn't.

This could be another part of some sick hoax. Or else the woman could be working for the person who'd hired these now-dead thugs. Because her timing was certainly suspicious, and she could be here to make sure she finished the job that her hired guns had started.

"Did the woman give you her name?" Karina asked.

Good question. One that Cord should have already asked. He needed to collect himself. Hard to do, though, with the adrenaline still pumping through him, and his body primed for the fight.

The cop shook his head. "I figured if she was your

mother, that you'd know her name. I also figured she had come here with you." He did another thumb hitch. "You want me to get her ID and question her?"

"No. I'll do it." In fact, Cord didn't want anyone else talking to her yet. After they were done, it was possible these uniforms would be arresting her.

"I'll clean up," Karina said, looking at the blood on her hands. "I'll be out there in a minute."

"Stay back here until I know what we're dealing with."

That clearly didn't do anything to put Karina at ease. But then nothing would at this point.

Cord didn't holster his gun when he went into the diner, and he spotted the woman right away. Not inside but rather standing at the glass door. He couldn't see much of her face because the diner's name, Tasty Eats, was etched on it, so he went closer.

She stood there wearing a dark blue dress, her nearly white hair pulled back. Not in a fashionable style, either. She looked old.

No, he corrected. She looked weary.

An emotion he completely understood, but Cord pushed it aside. He didn't want to feel any connection with this woman until he found out exactly who she was and why she was there.

With his gun still ready, he opened the door. She was looking down at the ground and was holding a purse in front of her like a shield. Cord snatched it from her, causing her to gasp in surprise, and he rummaged through it.

No gun.

Wallet, keys, tissues and some papers, all neatly arranged.

"Who are you?" he demanded, handing her back the purse.

The woman lifted her head then, their eyes connecting. He didn't see the resemblance as he'd done with Willie Lee, but he did *feel* something.

Hell.

He couldn't trust a gut feeling on something like this.

"You don't remember me," she said, sounding a little hurt by that. "Of course you wouldn't. You were hardly more than a baby. Your name was Courtland then, but we called you Court."

Court. No doubt what he'd been trying to say when the person found him in that gas station. His name had gone down on record as Cord. No last name because Cord hadn't remembered one.

"And your sister was Gabrielle," Sarah added in a whisper. "I didn't think you would remember me, but I'd hoped..."

Each word put him through an emotional wringer. Because they could be true. He cursed that feeling again. The tug deep within him that told him that this could indeed be his mother.

"I'm Sarah Prior," she said, extending her hand for him to shake.

He put out his left hand, without even thinking about it. Mainly because he couldn't take his attention off her. Then, he fired off a text to Jericho, asking for the sheriff to run a quick background check on the woman's name.

"May we sit down and talk?" she asked. "I have some things to tell you."

"And I have some things to tell you." Of course, he didn't sound anywhere near as friendly, and frail, as she did.

Cord got another look at that frailness when he stepped back, and she came inside. She was limping, and judging from the way she maneuvered herself, the limp had been with her for a long time. Maybe an old injury.

She sat down at one of the tables, glancing over at the detective who was watching them. "Will he arrest me?" she asked. "Will *you* arrest me?"

Cord had to relax his jaw muscles before he could speak. "What have you done to warrant an arrest? Did you hire those two armed men in the kitchen?" He didn't tell her they were dead. Because if she was behind this, she might think they were in there spilling their guts to the cops.

Her eyes widened, and her hand went to her mouth, muffling yet another gasp of surprise. "No. Of course not. I wouldn't do anything to hurt you. I love you."

A burst of air came from his mouth. Definitely not humor. "If you're really my mother, then you abandoned me at a gas station. That doesn't sound like love to me."

That put some tears in her eyes, and even though what he'd said was the truth, Cord suddenly felt bad about it.

There was some movement to the side. Karina. She stepped around the officer in the doorway, but she didn't come closer. Not until Cord motioned for her.

"Is she your mother?" Karina asked.

"The jury's still out on that. This is Karina Southerland," he said. Great. He was making introductions now. If this kept up, he'd be hugging the woman.

Much to his disgust, it was something he wanted to do.

"I'm Sarah." The woman shook Karina's hand, too. "Willie Lee works...worked for you."

"He did. And I don't think he's the Moonlight Strangler. I don't believe he could hurt anyone, and I've known him for years."

Well, since Sarah and Karina had brought it up, it was time to get this conversation moving. The cops likely wanted to start processing the scene and get them out of there for statements.

"Start from the beginning," Cord ordered her. And it was an order. "Tell me what happened. If you lie, or even if I think you're lying, you will be arrested." He had no idea what the charges would be, but he'd come up with something.

Sarah nodded, nodded again and then took a deep breath. "Willie Lee and I got married thirty-four years ago when I was pregnant with you and your sister. Samuels wasn't his last name then. It was Joyner. Willie Joyner. He didn't start using Willie Lee Samuels until, well, later."

That explained why no one had been able to find birth certificates for Addie and him, but there was no official name change on record for Willie Lee. However, he could have just started using the name without making it legal.

Cord would want to know all about that *later* part she'd mentioned, but he wanted to hear more of the beginning. He motioned for her to keep going.

"We were happy, for a while anyway," she finally continued. "Money was tight so Willie Lee took a lot of jobs. Sometimes, he had two or three at once. I complained about never seeing him, and I think that's what made him desperate. Because he got mixed up in something with some bad men."

"Money laundering?" Cord asked.

"Yes. I don't think he knew what was going on. Not at first. And then it was too late." She pulled one of those tissues from her purse and dabbed her eyes. "Things got bad. One of the men involved in that mess took Addie. He kidnapped her, and he did that to keep Willie Lee quiet."

That meshed with some of the things Addie had learned and remembered about some man taking her to a woman's house. Obviously, Addie hadn't been hurt, but she darn well could have been. It sickened him to think of that even now.

"How did you get Addie back?" Cord asked.

She tucked a strand of her hair behind her ear, twisted the tissue in her hand. "I'm not sure. Willie Lee worked that out. And we moved, he changed our last name and started a new life. Things were better for a while. And then *he* came."

"He?" Cord persisted.

Another breath. "I don't know who he was. A stalker. It started with hang-up calls and...escalated. He started leaving pictures of your sister, you and me. Pictures I didn't know he was taking. Some of them were taken from my bedroom window when I was dressing."

Karina winced a little. Probably because she had her own version of a stalker with Rocky and his club friends.

"And you never saw this man?" Karina asked.

"No. Not once. But I always got the feeling he was there, nearby. Once I even stood out in the yard and yelled for him to tell me why he was doing this. He didn't answer, and the following day he sent me some photos of mutilated animals."

Even though Cord didn't want to believe her, he did. About that part anyway. Cord could practically see her reliving what must have been a frightening time for her.

"Someone claiming to be the Moonlight Strangler sent me photos," Cord said. "One was of Addie and me on the porch with a woman."

"Yes, she was a neighbor lady, Ida Kincaid, who babysat the two of you sometimes. She was watching you while I had a doctor's appointment." Sarah shuddered, touched her mouth again. "When I came home, I found Ida's body in my bedroom. It was obvious someone had murdered her."

Cord didn't bother holding back the profanity, and he was about to jump down Sarah's throat about why she hadn't reported it to the cops. And he knew she hadn't because Cord had all the names of the Moonlight Strangler's known victims and even those who had similar MO's.

Karina shook her head, silently begging him to pull back on the anger, and she moved closer to Sarah and slipped her arm around her shoulders. That's when Cord realized Sarah was crying again.

"What did you do after you found the body?" Karina continued, and her voice was a lot calmer than Cord's would have been.

"The twins were outside playing, and I was afraid he was still in the house. So, I gathered up the children and drove off as fast as I could."

Cord didn't hold back this time. "Why didn't you go straight to the police station or call them before you left the house?"

"He'd cut my phone line, and I didn't have a cell phone in those days. And he'd left me a message. A note that said he'd kill me next...after he killed my kids."

Cord would have needed a heart of ice not to react to that. It felt like a sucker punch. Because Addie and he were those kids.

"I went to look for Willie Lee," Sarah explained after wiping away more tears. "But he wasn't at work, where he was supposed to be."

Maybe because he'd been back at the house taking that selfie and the photo of the dead woman.

But why would Willie Lee have pretended to be a stalker? If he wanted to torment his wife, it would have been much more effective if Sarah knew she was living under the same roof with a deranged man.

"I kept driving," Sarah went on. "Kept looking for him, and you had to go to the bathroom. It was dark by then, and I stopped at a gas station. You were too young to go into the men's room by yourself, so I took you in the women's bathroom. That's when he attacked me."

Sarah didn't jump right into the rest of that in part because the detective motioned for them to hurry things along. Probably because the crime-scene photographer had arrived and wanted to get started. Cord would have to take the woman to the local police station, but he had to hear the rest of this first.

"How did he attack you?" he asked.

"He turned off the lights and just came crashing through the door. He punched me hard. Both you and your sister started crying. But he kept punching me until he had me on the floor, and then he got me outside. I don't remember how. I was fading in and out of consciousness and terrified he was going to hurt my kids."

Yeah, that fear was real, too, and Cord got just a shimmer of a memory. Of the violence. But the images were gone before he could latch on to them.

"What happened then?" Karina prompted.

"I woke up in the trunk of his car. I could still hear my kids crying. Well, one of the kids anyway. My daughter. I couldn't hear Court...Cord," she amended, "and I thought the worst. God, I thought the worst."

So, maybe that's when Cord had been abandoned.

That felt like the truth, too, and he caught another image of him crying in the corner of the dirty bathroom. A roach had crawled across his shoes, and he'd been too scared and numb to react to it.

"I kept banging on the trunk," Sarah explained. "Kept trying to get out so I could help my kids. The man finally stopped out in the middle of nowhere. It was dark, no moon that night, and he was wearing some kind of mask. Like a stocking maybe. He dragged me from the trunk, and that's when I saw the blood on my baby girl's cheek. The bastard had cut her face."

Cord wished he'd been there. Yes, he was just a kid, three years old, but maybe he could have stopped it.

"I told my daughter to run. And she did. Thank God, she did. Because the man stabbed me, and he ran after her. I crawled into a ditch, trying to get up enough strength to help my baby. But the man didn't find her because she wasn't with him when he came back. I stayed hidden, and he finally drove off."

"And you survived," he concluded for her.

She nodded. "I got to a hospital eventually and gave them a fake name so he wouldn't find me. When I was back on my feet, I went looking for you."

No way could he keep the anger out of his voice. "You should have told the cops I was in that bathroom and that Addie was in the woods."

"I was stupid. The man had warned me he'd kill us all if I went to the cops. And by then, I'd read in the newspapers about you and your sister being found.

Not together, of course. But you were safe. So, I pretended to be dead so that he wouldn't try to use you to get to me."

Cord sat there, trying to process it, but he couldn't. However, he could see that this was ripping Sarah to pieces.

"I haven't seen you, your sister or Willie Lee since," Sarah added. Her gaze came to Cord's. "Has Willie Lee said anything about me?"

"He thinks you're dead, that you were murdered."

She didn't seem surprised by that. Probably because she'd just said she faked her death.

Karina leaned in, and she gave the woman one of the napkins from the table so Sarah could dry her eyes again. "Why didn't Willie Lee go to the cops with all of this?"

"I'm not sure. But it must have been something big to make him turn away from you. He loved you. Loved all of us." Sarah paused. "I want to see him. Do you think you can arrange that?"

Cord's first reaction was to say no, but he might learn a lot watching the two interact. "I'll work on it."

Sarah nodded, then stood, glancing around. "I need to use the ladies' room, and then I guess you'll be taking me to talk to the cops?"

"Yes," Cord answered without hesitation. All of this had to go on the record.

And then he had to call Addie.

"But you won't be able to use the bathroom here. Everything in the building will have to be processed."

Sarah eyed the gas station next door. "I'll have to go there, then."

When Sarah stepped outside, Cord got the attention of one of the uniforms. "Could you go with her and keep an eye on her?"

"Sure, but we're kind of busy here." It was obvious that the officer had more important things to do, but he did follow her and then stood by the door when Sarah went inside.

"You believe her?" Karina asked right off.

"Yeah." Cord thought Sarah was the real deal, and judging from the sound Karina made, so did she.

Cord's phone rang. Jericho, again. So he answered it right away.

"When were you going to tell me that someone tried to kill Karina and you again?" Jericho began.

It wasn't that Cord had forgotten about it. But meeting Sarah had pushed the attack to the back burner. "We're okay. I'll tell you about it when we make it back to Appaloosa Pass. In the meantime, did you find out anything about Sarah Prior?"

"Yeah," Jericho said. "Who the hell is she?"

It took Cord a moment to get out the answer. "I think she's my mother. Why? What'd you find out about her?"

"Not nearly enough. No records on her until twenty-nine years ago, so I'm betting that's not her real name. Or else she made sure not to leave any trace of herself so there'd be a paper trail. She's had various retail and clerical jobs. Nothing that stands out. But something must have stood out for you."

"It did. She's got a story to tell, and after Karina and I are back, you'll get to hear it, too."

Jericho stayed quiet a moment. "Does Addie know?"

"Not yet. Soon. Karina and I need to give our statements first. There are two deaths so that might take some time." It'd take more than *some time* to get that look out of Karina's eyes.

"Let me know if there's anything I can do," Jericho added, and he hung up.

Cord stood, helping Karina to her feet, and he went to the gas station bathroom to speak with the officer who was standing guard outside the door.

"The woman inside will need to go to your police station," Cord told him. "She has key information about an old murder investigation." Or soon it would be an investigation anyway. "Can you make sure someone gives her a ride there?"

Of course, he could have offered for Sarah to ride with Karina and him, but Cord really needed some time to try to make sense of this and clear his head. It wouldn't be long before Karina would be facing a serious adrenaline crash, and he needed to save some energy for that.

"I'll get somebody out here to give her a ride," the officer assured him.

Cord took a step, then stopped. He felt that too familiar feeling go down his spine. It was a feeling that he'd learned not to ignore.

Because it had saved him a time or two.

"What's wrong?" Karina asked.

Cord didn't answer. Instead, he hurried to the

ladies' room, and he threw open the door. It wasn't a large space, just two stalls, two sinks and a window, so it didn't take him long to see who was there.

Or rather who wasn't.

Hell.

Sarah was gone.

Chapter Fifteen

Sarah.

The woman's name and her story kept going through Cord's head, and the hot shower wasn't helping. Wasn't helping with the images, either. Images of those two thugs who'd tried to kidnap Karina.

Who were they?

That was still the million-dollar question, and in a perfect world, the cops would be able to pin this on someone in that stupid Bloody Murder club. But so far, there'd been no arrests, and both of the hired guns were not only unidentified, but they were also dead, so they obviously weren't talking.

That's why Cord and Jericho had beefed up security once again at the ranch. And it was the reason he kept his shower short. Karina had been asleep when he'd gotten up from the sofa, walked through the bedroom and gone into the bathroom, but he wanted to be there when she woke up.

In case she fell apart.

She had to be on the edge, especially after dealing with an adrenaline crash. When they'd finished giving their statements to the cops, they'd returned to the guesthouse. She'd showered, to get that blood off her hands, and had fallen right into bed. He'd checked on her several times throughout the night, but she hadn't moved from the spot where she'd landed.

But she had moved now.

Cord saw that the moment he stepped into the bedroom. Good thing he'd gotten some clean clothes from the closet before he'd hit the shower, or he would have walked in there stark naked.

Just the thought of it seemed to give his body some bad ideas.

Of course, seeing Karina gave him even worse ideas.

She was sitting up as if waiting for him. Her hair was tumbled all around her face and shoulders. And she was looking at him as if he might have the answers to the universe.

"I didn't hear you when you went into the bathroom," she said.

Cord shrugged. "You're a very deep sleeper."

"Yes." She flexed her eyebrows, repeated that *yes*. "Please don't tell me you watched me drool or anything."

"No drool." But then he thought they could use some lightness. "All right. Minimal drool."

It worked. She laughed. And it was so good to hear that. In fact, a first, and he hoped he got to hear her laugh and see her smile again.

The laughter didn't last long, though, and she studied him. "Bad news?"

"No. More like no news." Which some might say was a good thing. "There's still no sign of Sarah. No change in Willie Lee's condition. Mack's good to go, though. He's already home since the bullet went straight through and didn't hit anything vital. His girlfriend is giving him some TLC."

"That's good."

It was, but he could still hear the sadness in her voice. Mack had been shot by the men who wanted to get to her. Karina would see that as her fault.

It wasn't.

Maybe he'd be able to make her understand that.

"The San Antonio cops are going through Sarah's place," Cord continued. "They're hoping to find out where she could be hiding. And why."

He especially wanted to know the why.

He shook his head. "I don't understand it. Sarah came there to that diner. She spilled all those details of what'd happened to Addie and me. So, why did she just run off like that?" Climbing out of a window, no less.

"Maybe something spooked her," Karina suggested. "If you want to know what I think, though, I believe she's telling the truth. If you want to know for sure, I stole the tissue she'd used and put it in the pocket of my jeans. You can use it to do a DNA test."

"You did what?" But he waved off his question. He'd understood just fine. "I didn't see you take her tissue."

"I have sneaky fingers." With that, her gaze dropped

down to her hands. They were spotless, but she could no doubt still see the blood that'd been there.

"I killed a man," she whispered.

"You killed a *bad* man. That doesn't count." But he knew it counted. Knew that it would stay with her for the rest of her life.

Because he'd killed several bad men, too. He remembered each one of them. Their faces. The blood. And even now, it twisted his gut.

She reached for him, motioning for him to come closer.

Uh-oh. Cord figured he should just turn around and walk out. With the morning light slipping through the edges around the blinds, he had no trouble seeing every one of Karina's bruises. That cut, too. No trouble seeing the worry still in her eyes, either. The energy was practically zinging between them.

She was in no shape for what he was thinking about doing. Which meant he should leave her alone so she could try to get some more rest. Then he could fix her some breakfast and pretend that all was right with the world.

But he didn't walk out.

Instead, he gave trouble an engraved invitation and sank down onto the bed next to her.

Karina seemed to know exactly what that *invitation* meant because she reached out, pulled him closer and kissed him. It was a tentative kiss, not much of a real one.

So, Cord made it real.

Mindful of her bruises—but just as mindful of the need he felt in her—he dragged her to him and kissed her until there was no turning back.

She made a sound of pleasure. He'd heard it when he'd kissed her before, but it was lot hotter now than then. His body seemed to take that as a challenge, to make that sound even louder.

Stupid, yes. But it worked.

It felt as if Karina melted in his arms, and for the first time in ages, the flashbacks weren't in his head. Nor the images he wanted to forget. The only thing in his head was her.

He kept kissing her until they both needed more. It was easy to give more since she was half dressed. Wearing his T-shirt. He pushed it up and found a naked woman beneath.

Oh, man.

Just the sight of her nearly had him rushing this. His body was pushing him to take her now. But he could also see bruises on her rib cage and stomach.

Cord kissed each one. Softly. Gently. Then, he went lower and planted some not-so-gentle kisses there.

He heard her make that sound again. Louder. Much more urgently. Something he understood, but he wanted to linger a few moments longer. Wanted this to last a lot longer than his body was urging.

But Karina had a different notion about that.

She caught on to his arm, pulling him back up, his body sliding over hers to create some interesting friction. Yeah, this had to happen soon.

Karina must have thought so, too, because she yanked off his shirt. Cord went stiff for a second, bracing himself in case the scars killed the mood. They didn't. With her gaze connected to his, she lowered her head and kissed the scars, the way he'd kissed her bruises.

That did it. No more foreplay.

Karina and he were clearly on the same page about that because she went after his zipper. He was barefoot, so that made it easier to get his jeans off. Well, it would have been easier if she hadn't kept kissing him the whole time.

"Condom," he growled. He sat up, fumbling around to locate one in the nightstand drawer.

Later, he'd tell her that he hadn't put them there, that they'd been in the drawer when he first started staying at the guesthouse.

Later, he'd tell her a lot of things.

For now, though, he just managed to get on the condom, and he pulled her onto his lap so that his weight wouldn't put pressure on her bruises. She lowered herself, easing her body onto him until she took him inside her.

Cord had to take a second to catch his breath.

He'd known it would be special with Karina, but he hadn't expected to feel this. And he didn't have that thought for long. Every logical thought in his head vanished when they started to move together.

The face-to-face position was right for him to kiss her, so that's what he did. He took her mouth, touching her, moving her harder and faster against him. Time seemed to stop and yet speed up, too.

Until he felt her climax ripple through her body.

Cord hadn't needed much more incentive to finish this, but that was it. He gathered Karina into his arms, pulling her to him, and he let himself go right along with her.

IT WAS SILLY, but Karina kept smiling.

It'd been a long time since she'd been with a man, and never like that. Never. Which didn't make it just silly, it made her stupid.

Mercy.

She'd fallen in love with Cord.

How the heck could she have let herself do that? The answer didn't come even when Karina held her head under the shower for so long that her lungs started to ache for air. She'd hoped if she could just clear her mind, she might be able to get a handle on this.

But no handle.

Just some really great sex with a hot guy whom she loved.

Of course, he didn't feel the same way about her. How could he? Cord still thought she was defending a serial killer. Plus, many would say they didn't even know each other that well. They'd only met a month ago.

However, even after spelling all of that out, her feelings hadn't changed. And wouldn't. Yes, that broken heart was breathing down her neck now.

She finished her shower and dressed in yet more of Addie's borrowed clothes. After packing the things at her place, Karina had ended up leaving them behind when Cord and she had rushed out of there. Thankfully, someone had dropped off her meds, so at least she had those, but it was too bad she couldn't feel just a little bit normal in her own things. But after what'd happened the last time she was at her rental house, she wasn't eager to go back.

Karina made her way toward the kitchen, following the scent of coffee. And eggs. Cord was at the stove, cooking, while he had his phone sandwiched between his shoulder and ear.

"Yeah, I'll tell her," he said to the caller, and as if he'd known all along she was there, he glanced back at her. "Hungry?"

Not even close, but she nodded, smiled. Hoped that she looked seminormal. "What are you supposed to tell me?" she asked, motioning toward the phone that he was in the process of putting away.

"That was the ranch hand out at your place. Your horses are fine."

It was the second time he'd checked on them for her. Something she greatly appreciated. But when he turned, she saw something else in his eyes. Something she didn't believe had anything to do with what had just happened between them in the bedroom.

"Is something wrong with Willie Lee?" she asked, trying to tamp down her fears. Hard to do that, though, after everything that had happened.

"No word from the doctor yet." He paused, dished

her up some scrambled eggs. "This isn't exactly a good conversation to have over breakfast, but Jericho called. Harley's missing."

Well, that wasn't what she'd been expecting, and at first, she thought maybe it was a good thing. Especially after they'd learned about what had gone on with him in the army. But Cord's face told a different, less-than-happy story.

"When Jericho sent a deputy over to question Harley," Cord continued, "they found blood on the floor and no sign of him."

She thought about that for a second while she poured herself some coffee. "What about DeWayne? Is he okay?"

It was a reasonable question considering that two of their suspects, and his *mother*, were now missing.

"I don't know about okay," Cord answered. "DeWayne's alive, but he's talking to the press and bad-mouthing you, me, Jericho and anybody else who had anything to do with Taryn, the Moonlight Strangler or Willie Lee."

That was a long list of people, but it did lead her to a strong possibility. "You think DeWayne could have done something to Harley?"

Cord shrugged, and they sat down to eat. "I think anything's possible when it comes to those two. But it's also equally possible that the Bloody Murder club is behind this. Maybe they think I'm not working hard enough to clear Willie Lee's name, and if they give us enough copycat kills, I'll start to believe them."

Karina didn't get a chance to respond to that because his phone rang, and she saw the caller ID on the screen.

The prison.

Karina automatically moved closer. Not that it was necessary, though. Like before, Cord put the call on speaker.

It was Dr. Kenney.

"Willie Lee is stabilized now," the doctor immediately told them. "And while I still don't think it's a good idea for him to have visitors, he's insisting on seeing you two right away."

"Why?" Cord asked. "Did he get his memory back?"

"Yes. And he has something important to tell you."

That brought Karina to her feet. "What?"

"I wrote down the message word for word," Dr. Kenney continued. "Willie Lee says, 'I'm not the Moonlight Strangler, but I believe I know who is. I think it could be my brother.'"

Chapter Sixteen

Cord was a thousand percent sure that returning to the prison was a bad idea, but there was no way he was going to pass up the chance to question Willie Lee about this latest bombshell.

Or maybe it was just a lie.

After all, Willie Lee clearly loved Karina, and maybe this was his way of saving face with her by trying to make her believe he was innocent.

Of course, that meant bringing Karina with him, since she wanted to hear what Willie Lee had to say, as well. With the memory of the attack still so fresh in her mind, Cord had hoped she would stay at the ranch.

No such luck, though.

She was right by his side again as they started the process to get them through security.

"You're sure Willie Lee never mentioned anything about having a brother?" It wasn't the first time he'd asked Karina that. The first time had come shortly after the doctor's call, but Cord was hoping that the thirty-minute drive out to the prison had jogged her memory.

But just like before, she shook her head. "Then again, he didn't mention having kids, either," she reminded him.

Yeah, failing to tell anyone about a brother wouldn't have been much of a stretch after that. The man could have a dozen siblings for all Cord knew. Plus, there were plenty of other things that Willie Lee had omitted. Maybe he would blame that on his fuzzy memory, but he'd clearly remembered something.

I'm not the Moonlight Strangler, but I believe I know who is. I think it could be my brother.

Cord hoped Willie Lee had a name to go along with the accusation. And while he was hoping, maybe this mystery brother would be someone the cops could arrest before Karina and he even finished this visit.

"We should ask Willie Lee about Lonny Ogden, too," Karina added as they made their way through the second checkpoint. "I'm sure it's something Addie would want to know."

Cord certainly hadn't forgotten that name. Hadn't forgotten that he had another half sibling out there.

Well, maybe he did.

Lonny Ogden was flat-out crazy, and that wasn't just Cord's opinion. Ogden had been committed to a mental hospital, where he would likely spend the rest of his life, and he didn't know any more about his birth parents than Cord did. However, Cord, Addie and Willie Lee all shared DNA with Ogden. That was a fact. And it was enough DNA that it was possible Ogden was Cord and Addie's half brother.

Once they made it all the way back to the hospital

section, there was a guard there who motioned for them to take a seat by the nurses' station. "Dr. Kenney said for you two to wait here, that she'll be out soon to take you in to see the inmate."

Hell. Cord didn't want to wait. Or sit. He had way too much restless energy inside him so he started to pace. Karina paced with him.

"If you want to get your mind off this," she proposed, "we could talk about what happened this morning."

He doubted she was referring to the phone calls now. No. One look at her, and he knew this was *the talk*.

Of course, he'd expected it. Cord seriously doubted Karina was the sleeping-around type. Neither was he. But despite that, they'd landed in bed for exactly what he'd known it would be—great sex.

"Or maybe we won't talk about it," Karina added when she studied his face. "What, did you think I was expecting some kind of commitment? Because I'm not." She suddenly got very interested in looking at her fingernails. "I just wanted to make sure you're, well, okay with it?"

"Are you?" he asked.

She nodded. Patted his arm. The gesture was a little too quick, her smile a little too thin, which meant she wasn't okay with it. However, that wasn't what she said.

"It worked." She gave him another thin smile. "I got your mind off the rest of this mess."

He flinched a little at having sex lumped into *this*

mess, but she was right. Just the mention of the talk that he wasn't ready to have had gotten his mind off Willie Lee. But it didn't take long for the thoughts and questions to creep right back in.

So much to consider.

"What if Willie Lee really does have a brother?" Cord decided to say that out loud, hoping it would help him work through it. "And what if the brother was the stalker Sarah told us about?"

The one who'd cut Addie's face.

Something that still turned Cord's stomach. That ate away at him even more than Sarah or him being in danger when that stalker had taken them. Of course, now he had a new reason for his stomach to twist and knot because every time he looked at Karina, it was yet another reminder that he hadn't been able to stop this monster.

Heck, he didn't even know if they were dealing with two killers or one.

Karina nodded, and made a sound of agreement after she gave what he said some thought. "You're thinking this brother could also be the Moonlight Strangler? If it's not Willie Lee, that is," Karina quickly added.

It was exactly what he was thinking. And that took Cord back to their three suspects. "All of them, Harley, Rocky and DeWayne, are the right age to be Willie Lee's brother."

Maybe even Ogden's father.

And that meant they were all the right age to be the Moonlight Strangler.

"All of them have sketchy pasts," Cord went on.

"Harley failed that psych eval. Rocky is a serial-killer groupie. And DeWayne had a personal connection to at least two of the murder victims. Any of them could have started killing back when all that happened with Sarah."

And just kept on killing.

However, Karina must have seen a flaw in his theory right away because she shook her head. "Wouldn't Sarah have known if her own brother-in-law was the one stalking her and attacking her?"

"Maybe not. She said he wore a stocking mask. And besides, maybe Willie Lee and he were estranged."

There was another possibility, though. Perhaps Willie Lee knew exactly who—and what—his brother was and had maybe tried to keep him away from his family. After all these weeks of hating him, it was hard to paint Willie Lee in that kind of positive light, but it was something Cord had to consider.

"I should also have Jericho look in to Rocky's adoption. And have him check deeper into Harley and DeWayne, too. It's possible their birth records are fake."

Having that information would help to prove or disprove what Willie Lee would tell them, but it was also info that could be needed when they made an arrest.

Which would perhaps happen today.

Cord reached for his phone to make that call, only to remember that he didn't have his phone. Or his gun. It was prison policy that all electronics and weapons be left with the guards at the front entrance.

The door to the hospital room opened, and Dr. Kenney finally stepped out. She looked exhausted, probably because she'd been nursing her patient back to health.

Cord skipped the usual greeting. "Can we see him now?"

"Yes." The doctor motioned for them to come in.

Cord stepped inside, his attention going straight to the bed where he'd last seen Willie Lee. He was still there.

But he wasn't alone.

There was someone standing right beside him. *Sarah.*

KARINA CERTAINLY HADN'T expected to see Sarah Prior at the prison. Not after she'd sneaked out of the bathroom. But here she was.

And she was holding Willie Lee's hand.

Normally, Karina would have been pleased to see someone showing affection to a man she cared about, but she wasn't sure she could trust Sarah. Even if everything the woman had told them was true, that didn't mean she hadn't come here to try to hurt Willie Lee.

Still, that hand-holding had Karina rethinking that particular worry.

"I was going to have you wait until his other visitor left," Dr. Kenney explained, "but Willie Lee said he'd like to see all of you. She can't stay much longer, though. Personal visits are limited to an hour, and she's been here longer than that."

"Why are you here?" Cord's eyes were narrowed and fixed on Sarah.

Dr. Kenney, however, answered before Sarah could say anything. "She's been trying to see him for a while, but it took several weeks to get the paperwork approved for a visit."

"And who exactly did she say she was?" he asked the doctor.

That put some alarm on Dr. Kenney's face. "His wife. Is that not right? Did they make a mistake with the paperwork?"

"She's my wife," Willie Lee insisted. He sounded a lot stronger than he had the day before.

Good.

Because he needed to answer some questions. So did Sarah.

"No touching," the doctor said when she noticed the hand-holding. She aimed a look at the guard, no doubt a reminder for him to do his job and reinforce the rules.

Sarah eased back her hand, slowly, and Karina couldn't be sure, but it seemed as if both Willie Lee and the woman hated the loss of physical contact. Heck, maybe they were in love. Or at least had been at one time.

As the doctor had done with their other visit, she stepped to the back of the room and got busy writing on a chart. The guard, a huge bald guy, didn't budge, but he didn't especially seem interested in what was playing out in front of him, either.

"You sneaked off yesterday," Cord said, walking closer to the bed and with his attention still on Sarah. "Why?"

"The photographer was snapping all those pictures in and around the diner," Sarah answered without hesitation. "I was afraid my photo would turn up in the papers, and he's still out there. I didn't want him to see me."

He.

The stalker.

And maybe the killer, too.

Sarah's excuse was pretty weak, considering she was at the prison now, where lots of people could see her, but Karina would give her the benefit of the doubt. If Sarah had told them the truth, she'd lived her life on the run and in hiding for the past three decades. She probably didn't trust easily and didn't take many risks. Having her picture in the paper would have been a risk.

Besides, it wasn't Sarah she wanted to talk to today. That could come later. For now, both Cord and Karina turned to Willie Lee.

"Start talking," Cord insisted. "And this time, no memory lapses. I want a name and details."

Willie Lee nodded. "My brother's name is...was," he amended, "Nicky Burnell. I don't know what name he's using these days, but I'm betting it's not his real one."

Karina silently repeated the name, and she figured Cord was doing the same thing. But it wasn't a name that had come up in the investigations.

"Where is he?" Cord snapped.

"I don't know. That's the truth," Willie Lee added when Cord gave him a hard look. "My parents divorced when Nicky and I were just six. We're fraternal twins. Nicky went to live with my father—I never saw or heard from either of them again—and when my mother remarried, my stepfather adopted me, and I took his surname."

Cord huffed. "So, let me get this straight. You haven't seen or heard from your brother in fifty or more years, but yet you believe he's the Moonlight Strangler? And even though you've been struggling to remember things, you just happen to remember that?"

"I didn't piece it together until Sarah told me what went on that night you and Addie were taken, and it triggered the rest of the memories. I'm not sure why Sarah would have helped with that, but she did. Maybe because this is the first time I've seen her since all of that happened."

"Because I thought it best if I stayed away," Sarah whispered. "I didn't want to get him killed, and I didn't want that monster going after my babies again. I figured if I started looking for you, that it would make waves. And that he would find out about it."

She'd been crying again. Or maybe she'd never stopped. Her eyes were red and swollen, but even with that and this awful situation, every time her gaze landed on Willie Lee, Karina saw the love Sarah had for him.

Cord obviously didn't see the love, though. Or if he did, it didn't play in to his emotions right now. He was all lawman and looked ready to pick Willie Lee's story apart word for word.

"What did you piece together?" Cord asked him.

"That day he took Sarah and you kids, he left a dead woman at our house."

Cord nodded. "I saw the picture. There was a picture of you, too, and you were holding a knife. Want to explain that?"

The sigh Willie Lee exhaled was a weary one. "He made me pose for it. Held a gun to my spine and said if I didn't take it, he wouldn't tell me where Sarah and my kids were. Of course, at the time I didn't know that you'd been abandoned and that Addie and Sarah had escaped."

Cord's hands went on his hips. "You're still not giving me what I want here. Why would you think that was your brother?"

"Because of something he said to me when he was cutting me," Sarah explained. "He said this was to settle an old score with his brother. I wasn't sure what it meant at the time. Truth is, I tried to forget what he'd said. And what he'd done."

Even now, after all this time, Karina could see that just repeating those words shook Sarah to the core.

"What old score did he have to settle?" Cord asked, glancing at both Willie Lee and Sarah.

It was Willie Lee who answered. "I'm the one who told my mother about Nicky. He wasn't right in the head. He liked to torture and kill animals, and one night I woke up, and he was standing over me with a knife. I rolled away from him just as he stabbed the blade into my pillow. He was trying to kill me."

Like Sarah, there was plenty of emotion in Willie Lee's eyes and voice. Mercy. He'd lived with a nightmare, and it crushed her heart to think he'd held all of this inside.

"After that, my dad and mom divorced, and my dad took Nicky away," Willie Lee continued. "He was going to have Nicky admitted to some mental hospital in Mexico. He wanted to go where no one knew them, where they could get a fresh start."

And that could have happened. But she also knew that torturing animals was a red-flag warning.

"You know DeWayne," Cord said. "Wouldn't you be able to tell if he was your brother?"

Willie Lee shook his head. "I haven't seen my brother in twenty-nine years. People change. And Nicky and I were only six when he was taken away."

True. And the problem with Harley was that even if there'd been a brotherly resemblance, his scars would have hidden it. Besides, she wasn't even sure Willie Lee had ever actually met Harley or Rocky. Harley and Willie Lee had been at the same army training base, but that didn't mean they knew each other.

"Sarah had nothing to do with any of this," Willie Lee added. "She told me what happened that night. How he took her. How he hurt all of you. She was just trying to save you."

Since that no-touching rule didn't apply to Cord and her, and because Karina was pretty sure they could both use it, she took Cord's hand in hers. Their gazes met. Held. And she saw it all sink in.

Willie Lee and Sarah were telling the truth. They were his parents.

That meant the real Moonlight Strangler was still out there. Plus, he might not even be one of their suspects. Nicky Burnell could be anyone now.

And could be anywhere.

Cord used his free hand to scrub it over his face. "What about Lonny Ogden?"

Sarah and Willie Lee exchanged glances. "Wasn't he the man arrested for trying to hurt Addie?" Sarah asked.

"He was," Cord confirmed. "But Addie, he and I have enough DNA in common that he could be my half brother or some other close relative."

"Or Nicky's son," Willie Lee suggested. "I don't have any other siblings. No other children, either. And, yes, I'm sure."

Even though Willie Lee seemed so certain of that, Karina knew that Cord would check it out. He'd check out a lot of things. Hopefully, somewhere during that, maybe he'd be able to catch his monster and make peace with his parents.

And himself.

"Mrs. Samuels," Dr. Kenney said to Sarah. "You really do have to go now."

Sarah nodded, reached out as if to touch Willie Lee, but then she pulled back her hand at the last second. "I'll be back as soon as they let me see you again."

"Be careful." Willie Lee then looked at Cord and Karina and he repeated what he'd said.

Sarah started for the door, but Cord didn't budge. Clearly, he had some other questions on his mind. Ones that maybe he didn't want to ask in from of Sarah.

However, before Cord could say anything else, the overhead lights flickered. And then went out.

Just like that, they were plunged into total darkness.

Chapter Seventeen

"What the heck is going on?" the guard grumbled.

Cord was wondering the same thing. He automatically reached for Karina, pulling her closer to him, and he waited.

"The generator should kick in," Cord told her.

"It should have already kicked in," the guard said.

That sped up Cord's heart rate. Here he was with Karina in a prison, and he had no gun or phone, and something had gone wrong. Well, maybe. Cord held out hope that it was just some kind of malfunction even though he knew systems like this had backups for the backups.

"Everybody stay put," the guard ordered, and Cord heard him head toward the door.

"Shane, make sure no one's trying to get in," Dr. Kenney said to the guard.

"Nobody gets through me," the guard assured her. "You just stay where you are."

Cord didn't know this Shane, but he was big, and he was wearing a sidearm. That didn't exactly steady Cord's nerves because Shane could turn out to be dirty. Or someone could just overpower him, but for now Shane was their best bet at putting an end to whatever the hell was happening here.

"I got a really bad feeling about this," Willie Lee whispered. "Undo my restraints, please."

Cord had no intention of doing that, but Karina started fumbling around as if she might. "He's right. Something's going on," she agreed.

Cord was still holding out hope, and he also held on to Karina to stop her. He didn't want Willie Lee untied. Not just yet.

But Cord's hope quickly died when he heard the guard curse.

"The door's locked," the guard said. "It shouldn't be locked. And my communicator's not working, either."

Cord cursed, too. He didn't know the ins and outs of this prison, but the locks often required a code to activate them. No one in the room had done that, so maybe that meant someone had locked it from outside.

Could Sarah have done it?

She didn't seem the sort to be able to negotiate a prison's security system and block a communicator, but if she had indeed managed it, she could be trying to break Willie Lee out of here. Out of some of the scenarios his mind came up with, that was one of the better options. At least he could best Willie Lee and Sarah if it came down to a physical fight.

Shane would be much harder since he had that gun.

"No!" Dr. Kenney said. Not a shout for help. It was

more of a muffled whisper, and she could have just been reacting to the fact that the lights hadn't come back on yet.

"Dr. Kenney, are you all right?" Cord asked.

No answer.

He tried again and got the same result.

All right. So, she hadn't just been reacting to the door being locked. Something had gone wrong. But what?

Cord tried to pick through the darkness, but he couldn't see a darn thing. Even the machines next to Willie Lee's bed had quit working and no longer had the blinking lights. He wanted to go to the doctor, to try to help her if something bad was happening, but that would mean leaving Karina alone.

Since Karina had already been the target of three attacks, Cord had to consider that this might be attempt number four.

"Shane, can you see Dr. Kenney?" Cord asked. He asked the guard that for two reasons. Because he really did want to know if the doctor was okay, but Cord also wanted to know Shane's position. He didn't seem like a man who was light on his feet, but he didn't want Shane or anyone else trying to sneak up on them.

"No. I can't see her." Shane sounded scared.

There was no table next to the bed, but Cord grabbed the metal pole that was holding Willie Lee's IV. Not an ideal weapon, especially since the IV needle was still in Willie Lee's arm. But it was better than nothing.

Cord listened for shouts from outside the door. Maybe someone trying to get to them. But nothing.

Damn.

Was it possible that no one else at the prison knew what was happening in here?

"I'm gonna start pounding on the door," the guard said. "Nobody's out in the hall, but if I pound hard enough, they'll hear me."

However, he had no sooner said that when Cord did hear something. It was some movement coming from the direction where he'd last seen the doctor. He figured it was too much to hope that she'd just fainted and was now regaining consciousness.

"Is someone else in here?" Karina whispered to him.

"Maybe."

And Cord cursed himself for that. There were plenty of beds and machines in this room, and he'd been so focused on getting answers from Willie Lee and Sarah that he hadn't thought to search the place.

Maybe that wouldn't turn out to be a fatal mistake.

"I'm taking off Willie Lee's restraints," Karina said, her voice barely audible. Because her arm was touching his, Cord could feel her shaking.

This time he didn't stop Karina when she reached out for the straps that anchored Willie Lee's arms and legs to the bed. Whoever was in here with them could be there to kill Willie Lee. After all, if Willie Lee was dead, then the real Moonlight Strangler might get away scot-free. Cord wanted to give Willie Lee a fighting chance while at the same time protecting Karina.

That's why Cord worked with her to remove the restraints.

"So help me, if you try to hurt Karina, you're a dead man," Cord warned him. "I don't care if you're my father or not."

"I'd never hurt her," Willie Lee insisted. "Or you."

While the man sounded sincere enough, Cord would decide later if he was telling the truth. After the restraints were off, Cord moved Karina to the side, away from Willie Lee, while putting himself between her and the door.

But Cord had no idea if the threat would even come from the door. It could come from anywhere.

"He could have Sarah," Willie Lee said, his voice frantic now.

True. If the woman wasn't behind this, then the killer could have taken her again. That put a tight vise on his chest, but Cord couldn't borrow trouble. Not when they already had enough of it.

"Dr. Kenney?" Cord asked again.

There were more sounds that came from her direction. Sounds that Cord didn't want to hear.

Some fast clicks. Then a groan, followed by a heavy thud. Someone had fallen to the floor.

KARINA'S FIRST INSTINCT was to run across the room and help the doctor. But Cord held her back.

"It could be a trap," he whispered to her.

Mercy, she hadn't even considered that. Her mind

was racing, and it was hard for her to think. But she didn't need to think to know they were in danger.

Again.

What was going on?

"Shane?" Cord called out to the guard.

Nothing. Not at first anyway, but then she heard another groan. Definitely not from a woman. That was a man, and it was likely the guard.

"I think someone hit Shane with a stun gun," Cord said. "Did you hear the clicks?"

Karina had, but she hadn't known what it was. However, she'd had no trouble figuring out that someone had fallen. And that someone was probably Shane.

She tried to rein in her breathing. Her heartbeat, too. Hard to do, though, now that there was proof they were in trouble. Someone had taken out the guard, the biggest threat in the room since Cord wasn't armed.

Had Dr. Kenney done this?

Karina hadn't heard anything from the woman since she'd muttered that *no*, not long after the lights had gone out. But she could have been faking. Could have gotten in a stun gun, as well.

But had she?

Or was she incapacitated like the guard?

"My brother's behind this," Willie Lee whispered.

He'd moved, though Karina hadn't heard him do that. Judging from the sound of his voice, he was no longer on the bed. That was good if he had to fight back, but he wasn't in any shape for fighting. Just the day before, he'd had that seizure.

Well, maybe that's what had happened to him.

She was rethinking that. If Dr. Kenney was helping the Moonlight Strangler, then she could have given Willie Lee something to trigger a seizure or make it look as if he'd had one. If so, that meant the doctor heard everything Willie Lee had said to them. Everything Sarah had said, as well.

"Sarah," Karina whispered. She hadn't meant to say the woman's name aloud, but Sarah had left only seconds before the lights went out. Whoever was behind this could have taken her. She could be in danger.

"He'll kill her if he gets his hands on her." Willie Lee's voice was filled with pain and fear for his wife. "Sarah and I are the ones he wants."

"Well, whoever he is, he's not going to get us," Cord insisted. "Karina, stay close and follow me. I need to get the guard's gun. Willie Lee, stay here, and use this if you have to."

Since her eyes were finally adjusting to the darkness, she saw Cord handing off the IV pole to Willie Lee. That's when she noticed that Willie Lee no longer had the IV needle in his arm.

Cord pulled a fire extinguisher from the wall, and he unpinned his badge and handed it to her. "It's not much, but if you have to, you could maybe stab someone with it."

A sickening thought, especially since she had stabbed a man in that diner. Karina prayed she wouldn't have to do that again. Prayed also that they'd get out of this safely. Certainly by now someone knew something had gone wrong. The Moonlight Strangler couldn't have bought off every single guard and doctor in the place.

She hoped.

Cord and she started moving. Karina did as he said and followed him, staying close while they inched farther and farther away from Willie Lee. Maybe the killer wouldn't use this chance to go after him.

A sound caused Cord and her to freeze. A footstep, maybe. And once again, it'd come from the direction of Dr. Kenney. If she wasn't on the take, maybe she was trying to get to the guard, too. But then, who'd gotten to guard already?

"Get down on the floor," Cord said directly against her ear. "We'll crawl the rest of the way."

Maybe because he thought it would be harder for someone to shoot them that way.

With his badge still gripped in her hand, she went to her knees. Cord, too, and he didn't waste even a second getting them moving again.

The floor was tile. Hard and cold. And even though they were moving quickly, it seemed to take an eternity, but it was probably only a few seconds before they reached him. He was definitely on the floor.

Not moving.

But she could hear him breathing so he was alive. She also heard Cord when he cursed.

"His gun's gone. Someone took it."

No doubt the same person who was responsible for him being unconscious.

Before she could ask Cord what they were going

to do next, she heard the clicking sound again. The stun gun. Someone else groaned. But it wasn't Dr. Kenney or the guard this time.

It was Willie Lee.

Oh, mercy.

She looked behind her and saw him fall to the floor. Cord must have seen it, too, because he hauled her behind some of the machines and moved in front of her again.

It took her a moment to see him, but there was a man near him. Someone dressed all in black, and he blended right into the shadows and the darkness.

"Well, well," he said. "We all meet again. Isn't this special?"

God. "That's him," Karina blurted out. "That's the man who attacked me in the barn."

"The man who made the phone calls, too," he proudly admitted. "And sent those texts from God. But I didn't kill you in that barn, did I? No. Because that was just the appetizer. I wanted to finish the job here."

"Who are you?" she asked, her words mostly breath.

"I'm the Moonlight Strangler, of course. And I'm here to settle an old score. A couple of new ones, too."

She shook her head. "That's not the voice of any of our suspects."

The man laughed. "Confusing, huh? Well, I practiced using this voice for a long time, and I only use it for special occasions. Like now. Want to hear my real voice, Karina? How about you, Cord?"

"Yeah," Cord snapped. "I want to hear it. Just quit hiding behind that *voice* and tell me who you are."

He laughed again, stepping over Willie Lee, to move closer. And closer.

Until Karina could see his face.

Chapter Eighteen

Rocky.

Cord knew he shouldn't have been surprised. After all, Rocky was a suspect, but that only added another knot in his gut. Because Rocky had been living right next to Karina for days before he'd attacked her.

And now he was here, obviously ready to make another move.

But what move, exactly, did he plan on making? Or rather trying to make. Because Cord had no intention of letting him get to Karina again. Willie Lee must have thought so, too, because even though he was practically immobile from the stun gun, he was struggling to try to move toward Rocky.

His brother.

Cord could see it now. The resemblance. Something to do with the set of the jaw. Too bad he hadn't noticed it sooner. Maybe then he could have stopped him before it came down to this.

Rocky was armed, a gun in his right hand. The stun gun in his left. And he wasn't alone. Cord cursed again for not having checked out the room. Because a man stepped out from behind some of the machines in the back.

A hired thug, no doubt.

"I'm so sorry," someone said. Dr. Kenney. "I had no choice but to help him. He has my sister. He'll kill her if I don't help."

Well, that explained how Rocky and his henchmen had gotten into the prison with weapons. Or maybe they'd stolen the guns once they were inside.

"Quit your whining," Rocky mocked. "Your sister's fine. We've already released her. The effects of the drugs should wear off soon, and she'll probably call the cops. And if you play nice and don't make a scene, you'll live to see her."

The doctor made a hoarse sob. "You're not going to get any help," she said, and Cord realized she was talking to him. "He has guards on the take, too, and no one will be coming in here to stop this."

Hell. That wasn't what Cord wanted to hear. Of course, Rocky had had a month to set up all of this, and he'd almost certainly covered all the bases. Or at least thought he had. He was probably counting on the doctor to get him and his hired gun out of there when he was finished.

Rocky's plan almost certainly included another murder. His specialty. Since he'd been doing it quite well for decades.

"Doc, you need to get down face-first on the floor, and choose a spot where we can see you," Rocky instructed. "I can't trust that you won't do something to help them."

Judging from her glare, she would have tried to do just that. But the hired gun pointed his weapon at her until she did as Rocky had ordered. Dr. Kenney got on the floor.

Cord kept himself in front of Karina while he stared at this snake. "What do you want?"

Rocky made an isn't-it-obvious? huff. He tipped his head to Willie Lee. "I want him to pay for what he did to me. Because of him, I was locked up in a hellhole mental hospital for two years. Abandoned by our father. And then shuffled into foster care only to end up with idiot parents."

"Parents who gave you the money to do what you're doing now," Cord said.

Rocky shrugged. "There is that. Money allowed me some freedom, and they were happy to pay me off to get rid of me."

"The freedom to hire killers," Karina snapped. "How could you do this? I trusted you."

"Well, Karina-girl," he said, using the Moonlight Strangler's voice, "your trust was misplaced. But if you hadn't hired me, I would have found another way to get close to you. Once I learned you cared for Willie Lee that made you the perfect target. You still are. Because now Willie Lee will get to watch you die."

"Why?" Karina asked.

Because she was pressed against his back, Cord could feel her trembling. Could also feel the fierce hold she still had on his badge. It might come in handy since Rocky would almost certainly want to try to strangle her. That meant coming a lot closer. In a hand-to-hand battle, he could beat this idiot.

But not if his henchmen shot Cord.

That's the reason Cord kept Karina behind the machines and hopefully out of the line of fire. Of course, there was nothing he could do about Willie Lee.

His father.

It wasn't a good time for that to really sink in with Cord, especially since he might lose him before he even got a chance to work out his feelings for him.

It was the same for Karina.

Cord didn't need another reason to get them all out of this alive, but it was part of this.

"Why?" Karina repeated. Not a trembling whisper this time. It was a shout.

"All righty, then." Not the serial killer's voice but it was syrupy sweet. "I'll give each of you one question, just one, and then I get to play. I do like to take my time with that, and I don't want any talking when I start. Screaming is fine, though."

Since the dirtbag had offered it and since Willie Lee couldn't speak for himself, Karina asked the question they all wanted to know. "Did you plant Willie Lee's DNA at that crime scene?"

"No." And it wasn't hard to tell Rocky was irritated about that. "That was all DeWayne's doing, and before I killed him, he said it was to get back at Willie Lee. Of course, he whined and begged a lot before he made that confession."

DeWayne was dead. Cord wanted to believe that was all talk, but he doubted it. The Moonlight Strangler wouldn't have any trouble adding one more body to his list.

"I don't like people using me to get what they want," Rocky added. "And that's why DeWayne's dead."

"And now you want me dead, too," Cord added, "because I'm Willie Lee's son."

Damn. The panic crawled through Cord. *Addie*. Rocky might send one of his thugs after her, too. He prayed his sister was still safe at the ranch.

"You told Addie you wouldn't hurt her," Cord reminded him.

"Oh, and I won't. I'm not really interested in killing my own niece, especially after she managed to get away from me. And you, well, I left you in that bathroom because I didn't want to kill you, either. Of course, that's all water under the bridge now." He glared at Cord. "You've gotten in the way, and you'll pay for that."

Not if Cord could do something to stop it. But what? He still had the fire extinguisher, and he might be able to temporarily blind Rocky and the thug if they got close enough.

Rocky looked at Willie Lee, who was still struggling to move, and he kicked Willie Lee in the ribs.

"Don't you hurt him!" Karina snapped, and she would have bolted toward Willie Lee if Cord hadn't pushed her back.

"Don't make this easier for Rocky by going closer to him," Cord whispered to her. "And if the thug starts shooting, get down on the floor."

If Rocky heard what Cord had said, it didn't get his attention. He was still hovering over Willie Lee.

"Guess you won't get to ask your one question, big brother. So, let me try to guess what you would say if you could speak." Rocky tapped his own chin with the gun. "You want to know how I plan to get away with this. That's what good guys always ask the bad guys. Well, easy peasy. I got plenty of helpers, too, thanks to lots of money and some of the more malleable members of that murder club."

Rocky stopped, shifted his attention to Cord and glared at him. "But I have to say, I'm not happy about you killing so many of them. Good club members are hard to find."

"You got one of them, Scott Chaplin, killed by going back to that barn where you attacked me," Karina snapped. "And you must have had another club member with you that day because there was another shooter."

"Now, now. You've already had your one question, Karina-girl, and Scott was just a necessary casualty. We went there to get those photos and such, but it was too late. The cops had already found them. Besides, Scott was a problem child. You see, he got hurt that night, and it was his blood the CSIs found near the barn. Couldn't have him around after that. Killed the other club guy, too. Can't remember his name, but I didn't want anybody around who might have seen or heard something that day. They didn't know who I really was."

Ironic. The whole time they'd had the real Moonlight Strangler in their midst and didn't know it. And now, they'd died because of it.

Rocky shifted his gaze to Cord. "You got a question for me?" He tossed the stun gun on the bed and pulled a switchblade from his pocket. "Make it fast. I'm getting antsy. I need to cut somebody."

Cord didn't want to ask this piece of slime anything. What he wanted was a way out of this.

And he saw it.

Willie Lee lifted his hand just a fraction. Another inch or two, and he might be able to grab Rocky's foot and distract him. Just enough for Cord to launch himself at Rocky and the thug.

First, though, Cord had to give Willie Lee a few more seconds. He bought him that time with a question.

"How does Harley fit into all of this?"

Rocky pulled back his shoulder as if surprised by the question. "He doesn't. My men chatted with him, and he spewed some nonsense about Willie Lee maybe keeping a journal he wanted to get. Something that had to do with a business they were in a long time ago. I wasn't interested, so when Harley got away from my men, I didn't bother sending them to get him."

That explained why there was blood in Harley's place. And as for that old business, it was probably the money laundering. The statute of limitations had long run out on that, but Harley could have still wanted to get his hands on Willie Lee's journal if there was something to incriminate him in it.

That wouldn't have set well with Harley's wife and in-laws.

"I'm surprised you didn't ask about the other attack," Rocky said. "The one that happened a month ago where I got *you*." He smiled that sick smile at Cord.

"Didn't need to ask," Cord retorted. "You drugged both Willie Lee and me, cut me and took us to that church. You let me believe Willie Lee had set it all up so I would shoot him."

"Such a clever boy for figuring it all out," Rocky mocked.

Just thinking about that hurt Cord. Hell. He'd shot Willie Lee because that's exactly what Rocky had planned. In Rocky's sick mind that was probably the justice he wanted.

Willie Lee being killed by his own son.

And that had nearly happened. Somehow, Cord would have to learn to live with that. But first, he had to stay alive and get Karina, Willie Lee and Dr. Kenney out of this.

"Q and A is over," Rocky announced, smiling. He flicked open the switchblade and started toward Karina.

However, Rocky didn't make it but a step when Willie Lee latched on to the man's ankle. Willie Lee obviously didn't have much strength yet, but it was just enough to throw Rocky off balance. Rocky made a feral sound of outrage.

And that was Cord's cue to get moving. He hurried toward them.

But he didn't get far.

The thug took aim. And he pulled the trigger.

EVERYTHING HAPPENED SO FAST. One second Karina was standing behind Cord, and the next, he'd pushed her to the floor.

Not a moment too soon, either.

Because the gunman shot at them, and the bullet slammed into the concrete block wall where they'd just been standing. It wasn't a blast like normal shots. More of a swishing sound, which meant he was using a silencer.

Too bad.

Because if it'd been a regular shot, then someone would have heard it, and while Rocky had said he bought off some of the guards, he couldn't have bought off the whole prison.

Her heart was slamming against her chest now, and the sound of her pulse was thundering in her ears, but she had no trouble hearing Rocky's command.

"Kill them all," he shouted to the gunman. "I'll take care of my brother."

Oh, God. Rocky was going after Willie Lee. And Rocky had both a gun and a knife. Willie Lee was in no shape to defend himself, and she had to help him.

But how?

The thug was coming right at them, fast, and he maneuvered around the machines so that he could take direct aim at them.

But instead, Cord took aim at him.

Cord pulled the trigger on the fire extinguisher,

the white cloud of chemicals going right in the guy's face. He cursed and staggered back, but still managed to get off another shot.

The shot hit the floor right next to Karina, the bullet tearing into the tile and sending bits of it flying right at her. Karina automatically scrambled away from it, but Cord didn't. He lunged at the thug.

Cord rammed the fire extinguisher into the man's stomach as hard as he could. He rammed his body against him, too, and both Cord and the man crashed to the floor.

Karina hurried toward them. Or rather that's what she tried to do, but another shot came right at her. This one slammed into one of the machines. Metal hitting metal, and the bullet ricocheted, smacking into the wall.

And this shot hadn't come from the thug.

Rocky had fired it at her. And he quickly took aim again.

"Get down," Cord shouted.

Karina did, dropping down next to the machine Rocky's bullet had just hit. She couldn't see Rocky's face now, but she could see Willie Lee. He was bleeding. A cut to his head from the looks of it, and he was still struggling to move.

However, Rocky wasn't struggling.

He made another of those feral sounds and fired another shot. And he didn't stop there. She saw his feet running straight toward her.

God.

There was no place for her to go, and Karina

couldn't help but flash back to the other attack in the barn. Rocky had nearly killed her then before she'd managed to get away. Or maybe he'd allowed her to get away. So that he could kill her now in front of Willie Lee. That other attack could have been some sick mind game.

But this one sure wasn't.

Rocky was coming for her.

She got the badge ready, trying to position the sharp edges so she could try to stab him with it. She tried to ready herself, too. Karina brought up her hand. Just as Cord latched on to Rocky.

And Cord pulled him into the fray with the gunman.

Since both Rocky and his man were armed and Rocky had the switchblade, Karina had to do something fast or they'd kill Cord.

The fire extinguisher was on the floor now, but it'd rolled beneath the bed, not far from Willie Lee. There weren't any other weapons around so she hurried to Cord and looked for an opening so she could try to hit or kick Rocky or the thug.

Hard to do, though, with Cord in a fight for his life. Both Rocky and the man were bashing their guns against Cord, and it wouldn't be long before they managed to shoot or stab him.

Karina didn't think. She jumped in, her body landing on Rocky, and in the same motion, she struck him with the badge. He howled in pain and used his gun to backhand her.

It felt as if her head had exploded.

The pain shot through her, robbing Karina of her breath, but she could still see. And what she saw had her heart nearly stopping. Rocky was standing over her now. His face was bleeding, no doubt from the badge.

"You cut me," he growled, and he lifted his switchblade and came right at her.

Cord stopped him, again, slamming him down to the floor. It stopped Rocky but not the hired gun. He managed to pull the trigger again.

Karina felt a different kind of explosion in her head. And in her heart. God, had Cord been shot? Was he dead?

That got her fighting again. And she wasn't alone. Yelling, Dr. Kenney came off the floor, and she still had that clipboard in her hand. She hurried to the thug and bashed the clipboard against his hand and his gun.

The gun went flying, skittering across the floor, but he punched her, hard, and the doctor went flying backward. Karina could have sworn she heard the sound of bones breaking. However, she couldn't take the time to check on the woman because Karina saw something else that robbed her of what little breath she had.

Rocky was on top of Cord, and he had the knife to Cord's throat. The thug was there, too, bleeding, and while he no longer had his gun, he was big and could help Rocky kill Cord.

"If you move, he dies," Rocky said, glancing back at her.

She believed him. But if she didn't move, then they would all die anyway. Mercy, this was shattering her heart. She couldn't lose Cord. She couldn't.

"I'll go with you," she pleaded, hoping that it would get Rocky to move his knife. "You never wanted to kill Cord anyway, that's why you left him at that gas station."

Rocky's teeth came together. They were bloody, too. The blood had slid down from the cut on his face to his mouth. Ironic. Since the cut was similar to the one he'd given her.

And all his other victims.

Rocky's eyes were cold and flat when he looked at her. "No deal. Cord dies, then you."

He turned, probably ready to finish this, but since Rocky had been looking at her, he probably hadn't seen Cord's fist. Cord knocked the knife from Rocky's hand, and he punched him.

"No!" Rocky yelled. He staggered back, bringing up his gun. And aiming it at Cord.

But there was the swishing sound again. And Rocky froze. For a second or two anyway. Before he clutched his chest, and his gun fell from his hand.

Karina had no idea what'd just happened. Until her gaze slashed to Willie Lee. He was still on the floor, but he'd grabbed the thug's gun from beneath the bed.

And Willie Lee had shot his brother.

Rocky didn't fall, and he turned as if he might lunge at Willie Lee. But Willie Lee didn't let that happen. He pulled the trigger again. And again.

It took four shots before Rocky dropped to his knees and then collapsed.

But that wasn't the end of it. The thug was alive, and he came at Cord. However, he didn't make it. Cord grabbed Rocky's gun, and he fired.

No silencer on this one, so the shot blasted through the air. It was deafening. But effective. The thug dropped like a stone, and Karina only had to glance at him to know he was dead.

Karina hurried to Cord, praying that Rocky hadn't shot him. There was blood, but God, there was blood everywhere. She couldn't tell if it belonged to him, Willie Lee or Rocky.

"Stay back," Cord told her.

Both Willie Lee and he still had their guns aimed at Rocky. And she soon saw why.

Rocky was alive.

He was on his back and was laughing. Or rather that's what he was trying to do. He wasn't making much sound.

"You think this is over," Rocky said. His voice didn't have much sound, either, but it was clear enough that she had no trouble hearing him.

"It's over," Willie Lee assured him.

"Not a chance. Because one of my men has her, you see."

The chill that went through Karina was pure ice. "Her?" But she already knew the answer, and judging from Willie Lee's groan, so did he.

"Sarah," Rocky confirmed, turning his head to

look at Willie Lee. And Rocky used his last breath to finish that. "You'll never get to her in time to save her. Sarah will be my last kill."

Chapter Nineteen

Sarah will be my last kill.

Cord wanted to believe Rocky was lying, but he knew in his heart that the man wasn't. Rocky hated Willie Lee enough to take away something—anything—that he cared about.

And Willie Lee clearly cared about Sarah.

"You have to find her now," Willie Lee insisted. He was still too weak to stand, but that didn't stop him from trying. He caught on to the bed and tried to drag himself to his feet.

Cord glanced at Karina to make sure she was okay, but she was already running for the door. She started pounding on it before he even got there.

"Help us!" she shouted.

The guard that'd been subdued was moving now, too, and he tried to join them. So did the doctor, even though she wasn't 100 percent, either. There was blood on her face, and Cord was pretty sure the thug had broken her nose when he punched her.

Dr. Kenney grabbed the phone from the wall and demanded that someone get there ASAP. Now that she no longer had to worry about her sister, she was obviously doing her part to help.

But he needed a different kind of help from her.

"Rocky probably has Sarah somewhere here in the prison," Cord said to the doctor. "He would have needed a guard or two on his payroll for that."

She nodded. "He paid off two of them, and they should be right outside in the hall. That's where he told them to wait before Karina and you came in."

There was a reinforced glass panel on the door, and Cord looked out. He didn't see Sarah, but there was a guard, and he was backing away from the door while his gaze fired all around. He likely knew from the sound of the gunfire that he didn't have much time before other guards arrived.

Ones who weren't on Rocky's payroll.

Even though it was useless, Cord bashed himself against the door, trying to force it to give way. Sarah was out there somewhere.

His mother.

Rocky almost certainly had left orders for her to be taken away, or worse, if something went wrong. And it had. Rocky was dead. Cord had gotten damn lucky that Karina and Willie Lee were alive, but he might lose his mother before he even got the chance to know her.

He rammed against the door again, the pain from the impact jolting through his shoulder, and this time he heard the click of the lock. Not from anything he'd done. He glanced out into the hall again and saw the other guards storming toward them. One of them had no doubt disengaged the lock.

Cord rushed out into the hall, and one of the guards latched on to him. Only then did he remember he didn't have his badge.

"He's DEA Agent Cord Granger," Karina said, holding up the badge. There was blood on it, but the guard must have seen enough of it to let go of him.

Cord went in search of that guard he'd spotted earlier. He had to find Sarah. He had to get to her in time.

"There's a woman missing," Karina explained. "She's probably somewhere nearby, and her life is in grave danger. You need to help Agent Granger find her."

Even though Cord was making his way up the hall, he heard the doctor step in to help with the explanation. Hopefully, she would help Willie Lee, too. Cord wasn't sure how bad his injuries were. Maybe not enough to kill him.

Hell. He could lose both his parents today.

Cord still had the thug's gun, and he readied it as he threw open the first door he reached. It was an office of some kind, and it was empty.

He refused to believe the guard had managed to get out of there with Sarah, but Karina was taking care of that, too. She was calling out for someone to check the parking lot and to stop anyone from leaving the building. The prison was probably on lockdown now anyway, but that would help in case the guard had already made it that far.

Cord hurried down the hall, checking each room.

All empty. Probably Rocky's doing. Dr. Kenney had said Rocky had paid off two guards, and those two had probably made sure the hall and offices were cleared so their psycho boss could go on a killing spree.

"Search each room," Cord told the guards who were trailing along behind him. "And be careful. The two men who have her are guards, too, and they'll both be armed."

Cord reached the next door. Not closed like the others. It was wide-open, but he didn't go barging in there. He stayed to the side of the jamb and peered around it.

Sarah.

She was alive. For now. But there were indeed two guards holding her at gunpoint. The men were having what appeared to be a whispered argument, and Cord could practically smell the panic on them. They obviously hadn't thought things would play out like this.

"If you hurt her, you both die," Cord warned them, and he didn't leave any room for doubt in his voice or the glare he shot at them.

The man on the right cursed, and he threw down his gun, putting his hands in the air. Cord took aim at the other one, and the guy seemed to have a fast debate with himself. Before he, too, surrendered.

Cord hurried to Sarah and pulled her from the room so the guard could go in and restrain Rocky's hired thugs.

"You're hurt," Sarah said, her breath gusting.

He didn't want to be touched by her concern, but

he was. And Cord was glad for both her concern and what he was feeling. It felt as if some ice had melted from his heart.

"I'm okay." That was all Cord managed to say before Karina came rushing out of the hospital room.

"It's Willie Lee," she said, motioning for them to come. "Hurry."

KARINA TRIED NOT to look as if she was panicking. There were already enough panicked and worried looks in the waiting room, what with Addie, Sarah and even Cord, and she didn't want to add more. But inside she was definitely panicking.

Before Cord and she had come here today, there had already been so many nightmarish memories in her head, but now she had a new set thanks to Rocky trying to kill them. And Willie Lee collapsing after Cord had gone off to find Sarah. Cord had succeeded, thank God, but Willie Lee might not be so lucky.

Because he'd had another seizure and then collapsed.

Dr. Kenney had been right there to help him and had called in another doctor as well, but it'd been an hour now with no news.

Cord had used that hour a lot better than she had. He'd gotten the guards to bring him his phone so he could make lots of calls, including one to Addie, and she'd rushed there. She was sitting next to Sarah now. They were holding hands and talking. Not quite looking like mother and daughter.

Not yet anyway.

But as an outsider, Karina could see the new bond forming. Not just between Addie and Sarah, either. Cord was included in that, too. He'd gotten his mother a cup of water and had stayed by her side until Addie arrived.

Of course, he'd kept Karina close.

In a way.

He hadn't really talked to her, but he had wiped some blood off her face. She had no idea whose blood it was, and she'd done the same thing to Cord. They had some more bruises, but that was minor stuff compared to what could have happened.

And what could have happened was that Rocky could have killed them all.

They still might not have come out of this unscathed, though, because Willie Lee might not make it. It sickened her to think that after waiting all these years he might not get to spend any time with his wife and children.

Cord looked up from his call, his gaze connecting with Karina's, and he made his way to her. He dropped down into the seat next to her, ended the call and put his phone away. She figured he was about to ask her the same thing everybody else had asked.

Are you okay?

But he didn't.

He kissed her.

Karina went stiff from the shock. His sister and mother must have been surprised, too, because they quit talking. Or at least Karina thought maybe they had. After the kiss went on for several long moments, Karina wasn't sure she could hear anything.

Mercy, though, she could feel.

Cord eased back, met her eye to eye again. "Better? Because I'm better now."

Karina hadn't thought it possible, but she actually smiled. "Better."

But that feeling of heat and euphoria didn't last nearly long enough. The memories came flooding back. So did the tears, and she tried to blink them away.

"I'm so sorry," Karina said. "This is all my fault. If I hadn't hired Rocky, he—"

"He would have found another way to get to Willie Lee. And you. You heard Rocky. He was crazy and obsessed with getting back at his brother. If you hadn't hired him, he might have just killed you on the spot."

Cord cursed himself when she shuddered at the thought of Rocky getting his hands on her. But Cord was right, and it was something she needed to hear.

Still…

"I wish I'd figured it all out sooner," she said. "If I'd known he was the Moonlight Strangler, I maybe could have stopped him."

Cord frowned. And kissed her again.

"Do you two need to get a room?" Addie teased when the kiss went on a long time.

Cord broke away from her, smiling, but he gave his sister a very brotherly scowl. "I seem to remember seeing Weston and you kiss each other's lights out."

Addie nodded, readily acknowledging that. "My husband and I kiss a lot. And we're just as much in love as you two obviously are."

Cord froze. Karina did, too, but for a different reason. Because for Karina it was the truth. Cord, however, was probably nowhere near the *L* stage. And might never be.

A thought that broke her heart.

Cord, however, didn't get a chance to say anything because his phone rang again, and she saw Jericho's name on the screen. He didn't put it on speaker and instead stepped out into the hall to take the call.

Addie immediately motioned for Karina to join Sarah and her, and while she hated to intrude on a family moment, Karina finally went when Sarah motioned, too.

"I have two very strong, smart and wonderful kids," Sarah said. She also had tears in her eyes again. "I hope I get to make up some lost time with them."

"You will." Addie dropped a kiss on Sarah's cheek, and Karina saw the woman's face practically glow. "And once Willie Lee's fine and out of this place, we can go on a picnic together or something."

It seemed like such a, well, normal thing to do, and Karina wanted to hug Addie just for suggesting it. She didn't know Cord's sister that well, but she hoped she could spend more time with her.

Of course, it was just as likely that Karina would never see her again after today.

The door opened, and the three of them went to the edges of their seats. But it was Cord, not the doctor. Karina went to him in case he'd learned something bad that he was going to have to break to Addie and Sarah.

"It's not bad news," Cord told her right off. "Dr. Kenney's sister is all right. Rocky told the truth about that. She was drugged but wasn't hurt."

That eased some of the pressure in Karina's chest.

"But Rocky also told the truth about DeWayne," Cord added a moment later. He slipped his arm around Karina's waist and moved her several feet away from the other women. "The cops found his body."

So, the man was indeed dead. It was hard for her to feel sorry for the person who'd set Willie Lee up to take the fall, but DeWayne hadn't deserved to die. Instead, he should have been sent to prison for a long, long time.

"And Harley?" she asked.

"Alive," Cord answered. "Jericho's bringing him in for questioning about that money-laundering scheme. Now that the cat's out of the bag on that, there'll be no reason for Harley to try to cover it up."

Which meant there'd be no reason to come after her. Not that he had ever done that. No, Rocky had been responsible for those attacks and heaven knew how many murders.

"The SAPD is tearing apart the Bloody Murder club," Cord went on. "All the members are being arrested as accomplices to murder. That way, they can keep them behind bars until they sort out who was really working for Rocky and who wasn't."

Good. She didn't want any of Rocky's hired thugs on the loose.

Cord turned her so they were facing. "Are you really in love with me like Addie said?"

She nearly got choked on the breath she sucked in, and it took her a moment to realize he was serious, that he wasn't just teasing her.

Karina could only go two ways with this. She could tell the truth or she could give Cord an out. After all, he might feel he had to be with her just because of what they'd been through.

She went with the truth.

"Yes," she said. "I'm in love with you."

She braced herself for any and all reactions. Cord might tell her that she'd lost her mind. But he didn't. That's because the door opened, and this time a doctor came into the room. Not Dr. Kenney. She was likely getting her own medical attention for that broken nose.

"I'm Dr. Litton," the man said.

Addie took hold of Sarah's arm, and the two stood together. Waiting with their breaths held. Karina was doing the same thing.

"Willie Lee did have another seizure," the doctor explained, "but we believe it was a side effect from the drug that the man forced Dr. Kenney to give him. We also had to do some surgery. He'd been stabbed in the side."

Mercy. Karina hadn't even seen that happen, but it was no doubt from Rocky's switchblade.

Sarah touched her hand to her mouth to steady her trembling mouth. "How is he?"

"He'll make it. He just needs some recovery time."

The relief was instant, and Karina found herself in the middle of a sea of hugs. Smiles, too.

"From what I understand," the doctor went on, "the charges against him will be dropped, and when that happens, Willie Lee will be transferred to a civilian hospital. In the meantime, he wants to see all of you. You've got five minutes."

Not much time at all, and Karina considered staying put so that Cord, Sarah and Addie could have a family reunion. But Sarah took hold of her left hand. Cord, her right. And they followed the doctor into a recovery room.

Willie Lee was awake, but like Cord and her, he had some fresh bruises, as well. And of course, that stab wound. If Rocky had had just a few more seconds...

But she cut off that thought.

Rocky hadn't gotten those extra seconds because Cord and then Willie Lee had stopped him.

They went closer to the bed, Willie Lee reaching for each of them. He pulled Sarah closer for a kiss on the cheek. He did the same to Addie. And Cord.

Then her.

"I've always thought of you as one of my own," Willie said, giving Karina's hand a squeeze. "Now, I have two daughters. And a son."

"A grandson, too," Addie reminded him. "You'll get to meet him when you're better."

"I'm already better," Willie Lee assured her. He smiled at his wife. Then, winked at her. The levity was nice, but his expression soon turned serious. "I'm so sorry about all of this."

Cord huffed. "Karina's been apologizing, too. And Sarah…Mom," he amended. The word seemed a little stiff, but the look Cord gave his mother was anything but. Karina was betting within a month, they'd all be a real family.

Well, minus her.

"The doctor said five minutes," Karina reminded them. "I'll wait outside so you can have a few minutes together."

She turned to leave, but she didn't get far.

Cord caught up with her before she could make it to the door.

"Considering you just told me that you loved me," he said, "I think that makes you eligible for family status."

The others nodded, all agreeing. But Karina shook her head. "The love part has to be mutual for that to happen."

"Oh, it's mutual, all right." And he kissed her again.

It was a wow kiss. One of those that she felt from her head all the way down to her toes, which pretty much described any and all kisses that she got from Cord. He left her breathless and wanting a whole lot more.

Including the words that went along with that "it's mutual, all right."

She stared at him so long that he must have figured it out. "I love you, Karina," he said.

Well, that took care of the rest of her breath. So did the other kiss he gave her.

"Please tell me there's a marriage proposal that goes with all that kissing," Addie teased.

Karina had no such expectations. That's why she was stunned with what Cord said.

"We haven't had a date yet," Cord reminded his sister. "But give me a month to wine and dine her." He put his mouth right against Karina's ear and whispered, "And so I can get you in my bed again. After that, it's one knee, a ring and the question—will you marry me. How does that sound?"

Perfect. And Karina managed to say that to him, too. It was all perfect. But Cord made it even more so by pulling her into his arms for a kiss.

* * * * *

USA TODAY *bestselling author Delores Fossen's*
highly popular miniseries
THE LAWMEN OF SILVER CREEK RANCH
returns later this year with LANDON.
Look for it wherever
Harlequin Intrigue books are sold!

SPECIAL EXCERPT FROM

(H) HARLEQUIN

I N T R I G U E

*After witnessing multiple attempts to kill sexy
Stealth Operations Specialist Becca Smith,
Navy SEAL Quentin Lovett offers to cover her
six while she tracks down her father's killer.*

*Read on for a sneak preview of
A NAVY SEAL TO DIE FOR,
the third book in Elle James's thrilling quartet
A SEAL OF MY OWN.*

The door at the end of the train car opened and a man stepped through. Becca's pulse leaped. She reached out and gripped Quentin's leg. "Speak of the devil. He's headed this way. We need to hide. Right now." She shrank against Quentin's side, trying to get out of sight of the man heading directly toward them.

"Kiss me," Quentin urged.

"What?" She shot a glance at him. She'd wanted to kiss him all day long and wondered if he'd ever try to kiss her again. "Now?"

"Yes, now. Hurry." He swept the cap off her head, ruffled her hair, finger-combing it to let it fall around her shoulders in long, wavy curls. Then he gripped her arms and pulled her against him, pressing his lips to hers. Using her hair as a curtain to hide both of their faces, Quentin prolonged the kiss until Ivan passed them and walked through to the next car.

When the threat was gone, Quentin still did not let go of Becca. Instead, he pulled her across his lap and deepened the kiss.

Becca wrapped her arms around his neck. If Ivan came back that way, she never knew. All she knew was that if she died that moment, she'd die a happy woman. Quentin's kiss was that good.

The train lurched, throwing them out of the hold they had on each other. Becca lifted her head and stared around the interior of the train car. For the length of that soul-defining kiss, she'd forgotten about Ivan and the threat of starting a gunfight on a train full of people. Heat surged through her and settled low in her belly, and a profound ache radiated inside her chest. She wanted to kiss Quentin and keep kissing him. More than that, she wanted to make love to him and wake up beside him every day.

But she realized how impossible that would be. They were two very different people who worked in highly dangerous jobs, based out of different parts of the country. Nothing about a relationship with Quentin would work. She had to remind herself that he was a ladies' man—a navy guy with a female conquest in every port.

Don't miss A NAVY SEAL TO DIE FOR,
available October 2016 wherever
Harlequin® Intrigue books and ebooks are sold.

www.Harlequin.com

Turn your love of reading into rewards you'll love with
Harlequin My Rewards

THE WORLD IS BETTER WITH

Romance

2346

Harlequin has everything from contemporary, passionate and heartwarming to suspenseful and inspirational stories.

Whatever your mood, we have a romance just for you!

Connect with us to find your next great read, special offers and more.

f /HarlequinBooks

🐦 @HarlequinBooks

www.HarlequinBlog.com

www.Harlequin.com/Newsletters

❖ **HARLEQUIN**®

A *Romance* FOR EVERY MOOD™

www.Harlequin.com